THE China TATE SERIES

PROJECT BLACK BEAR

LISSA HALLS JOHNSON

PUBLISHING

Colorado Springs, Colorado

For my own Little Bear

*With special thanks to Mom and Dad
whose accidental research on bears
was crucial to this book.*

PROJECT BLACK BEAR

Library of Congress Cataloging-in-Publication Data
Johnson, Lissa Halls, 1955–
    Project black bear / Lissa Halls Johnson.
        p.   cm.
    Summary: China and Deedee must face the consequences of
their disobedience when they defy camp rules by feeding the bears.
    ISBN 1-56179-283-7
    [1. Camps—Fiction.   2. Christian life—Fiction.   3. Obedience—
Fiction.]   I. Title.
PZ7.J63253Pr   1994
[Fic]—dc20   94-12188
                                                         CIP
                                                          AC

Published by Focus on the Family Publishing,
Colorado Springs, Colorado 80995.
Distributed by Word Books, Dallas, Texas.

The author is represented by the literary agency of Alive
Communications, P.O. Box 49068, Colorado Springs, CO 80920.

This is a work of fiction, and any resemblance between the
characters in this book and real persons is coincidental.

Editor: Deena Davis
Cover Design: Jim Lebbad
Cover Illustration: Paul Casale

Printed in the United States of America
94 95 96 97 98 99/10 9 8 7 6 5 4 3 2 1

CHAPTER ONE

FROM CHINA JASMINE TATE'S PERSPECTIVE, the log bed and simple wood dresser stuck to the ceiling of Deedee Kiersey's room. Deedee seemed to hang by her hiking boots, but her hair—wildly curly and deeply red—floated uncontrolled about her head as usual. China's tawny hair, on the other hand, hung away from her head, sweeping the hardwood floor. "Hurry up, Deedee!" China begged. "My eyeballs are going to pop. Or my head's going to explode. Or something equally disastrous."

"Oh, stop it. You're fine," Deedee told her. "Hold still; it won't take long." Deedee brushed China's hair with long, firm strokes, her left hand gathering the hair as the brush smoothed the crinkles from it. She took a violet terry band and wrapped it around China's hair. "Okay. Now I want you to sit on the bed."

China unfolded herself and the ceiling turned back into the floor. She could feel the blood rushing out of her face. As she stood, she caught a glimpse of herself

1

in the mirror. Hair sprouted out of the top of her head. "Cute, Deedee, real cute." China reached for the purple band to yank it out.

"No, wait," Deedee pleaded.

"You're trying to make me look like a dork." China bobbed her head as the "fountain" splayed hair in all directions. "And succeeding, too."

"Sit," commanded Deedee.

China sat on the edge of the bed.

Deedee stood in front of her, the plaid shirt so close to China's face that the blues and greens blurred together. "Now I can't breathe," complained China. "I'm getting flannel hairs up my nose."

"Be quiet!" Deedee said, tugging slightly at China's hair.

China could see nothing except elbows moving up and down in her peripheral vision. A fine, watery mist shushed out of a spray bottle, some of it landing on China's bare arms. She shivered slightly.

"Ow!" China said as something pulled tiny strands of her hair.

"Sorry. I'm almost done."

China's head felt tight. "Are you giving me a face lift or what? I can't blink."

Deedee ignored her. After a moment more, she stood back to admire her work. "Perfect."

China stood and looked in the mirror. "What did you do to me?"

"Oh, stop. You'll like it tomorrow."

"In the meantime, it looks pretty stupid." China put her hand to her head. "Socks? You put socks in my hair?"

"Yeah. They make the prettiest curls this side of the beauty salon."

China looked unconvinced. "Says who?" She turned, looking over her shoulder, trying to see the back of her head.

"My mom. Her mom used to put Mom's hair up in socks. Or rags. You should see my mother's pictures."

"I think I should. I don't want to look like a total geek tomorrow. Rick will laugh me out of the kitchen."

"Magda won't," Deedee assured her.

"That's because Magda doesn't see anything except a person's heart. So when it comes to something looking geeky or not, Magda doesn't count."

"Okay, so Magda doesn't count. But you won't look geeky. Trust me."

China flopped across the bed. "Show me the pictures."

"We'll have to go to the living room. Mom's made a rule about pictures being in the back rooms. The little kids tend to rip the ones they like out of the books."

"What? You rip out the pictures, too?"

"No. Mom figures I can be a good example to the little kids. So the same rules apply to me as to them."

"Eeww. What a pain."

"Yeah."

The girls left Deedee's room and walked down the

narrow hallway to the comfortable living room. Mrs. Kiersey sat on the sofa, Deedee's two-year-old sister, Anna, in her lap. Five-year-old Eve sat snuggled under one of her mother's arms as Mrs. Kiersey read *Green Eggs and Ham*. As China and Deedee entered, all eyes looked up from the book. Eve pointed at China's head. Delighted, she started to giggle. "You've got socks on your head! China, why do you have socks on your head? You're supposed to put them on your feet."

"Your brilliant sister put them there." China jammed her hands on her hips and pretended to look mean. "And I don't want to hear another word out of you about the socks, or the tickle monster will have no choice but to launch a ruthless attack."

Eve clapped her hand over her mouth.

"Socks," Anna said, then jammed her thumb in her mouth.

"The same for you, young lady!" China wagged her finger playfully.

Anna pulled her thumb out of her mouth. "Socks."

China ran to her, tickling fingers wiggling at her all the way. Anna screamed with delightful anticipation. When China's fingers found their mark, Anna screamed louder while Diana Kiersey held the book out of the way. Then Eve shouted "SOCKS!" and China attacked her. Back and forth she went from one shrieking little girl to another. "Don't you say that word!" She warned them.

"Socks!" they squealed in return.

Diana Kiersey looked at her eldest daughter and smiled. "Can't you control your friend?" she called above the clamor.

Deedee shrugged her shoulders. "It's all your fault. If you'd never told me about the socks, this never would have happened."

Pretty soon Diana Kiersey slipped away while the whole gang, including Deedee, raced around the living room. The little girls hid behind the sofa and chairs, under a table, and covered themselves with the rug. The big girls played right along.

"Okay!" Diana Kiersey said, returning to the chaotic scene, catching a falling lamp in one hand. "Popcorn and cocoa for all well-behaved young ladies."

"I guess that leaves you out," teased China as she poked Deedee.

"You started this," Deedee reminded her.

"You did," insisted China. "The socks were your idea, not mine."

Deedee's face fell as she looked at China's hair. "You've ruined my artwork."

China looked into the mirror over the fireplace. Wisps of tawny hair hung down. The purple band had slipped down on one side of her head. The socks clung to her hair, but drooped sadly in all directions.

"We'll do it over," Deedee said.

"Not so fast, girl. I'm checking this out with your mother first."

"Fine."

Around the table, the sound of crunching popcorn replaced the earlier screams and teasing. Anna sipped a cup of cold chocolate milk. She watched Eve carefully, then made faces to try to match Eve's as if her cocoa were as hot as the others'.

"Diana," China said, popping an extra buttery piece of corn in her mouth. "Deedee swears this is the best way to curl hair. I don't believe it. I think she's only trying to have a good laugh. After all," China insisted, pointing at Deedee's natural curls, "what would she know about how to curl hair?"

"Wait here," Diana Kiersey said. She returned a moment later with a photo album. "Look." A young girl, who looked a lot like Deedee, stared toward the invisible camera. In one photo she had pieces of cloth sticking out from her head in all directions. A skinny girl, the cloth gave her a scarecrow appearance. In the next picture, the cloth had disappeared. The young girl wore a brightly flowered dress. Her hair fell in soft waves across her shoulders. In the next photo, she had turned around. The large, full curls hung down her back.

China looked up at Diana. "You really aren't kidding!"

Diana shook her head. "My hair wasn't as curly as Deedee's. It had some body to it, but it never quite looked right. Back in my mother's day most of the girls wore socks or rags to bed. When I went to college

I realized that if I put all my hair on top of my head, then rolled it in just a couple of socks, it took less time and didn't leave any kind of ridge in my hair at all." Diana lifted China's stray clumps of hair that had fallen from place. "I don't know how yours will work. Your hair is awfully straight. But it's worth a try."

China looked at Deedee, who grinned in triumph. "I told you to trust me."

"It still looks goofy," China insisted, trying to save a remnant of her pride.

"So? Who's going to see you?"

China glared at her for a moment. "Okay. I'll let you try."

"Socks," Anna said and giggled. When all eyes turned to her, she quickly popped her thumb into her mouth and pretended she'd said nothing. They all laughed.

China and Deedee put the girls to bed while Diana cleaned the kitchen. Without paying too much attention, China heard the phone ring, the mumbled conversation, and the phone replaced in the cradle. When the girls had prayed with the little ones and kissed them each on the forehead, they tried to leave. But Eve insisted they sing a song to help them go to sleep. "Song," Anna said.

The girls looked at each other.

"'Eyes on Jesus'," Eve requested.

"Jesus," Anna agreed.

"Do you know that one, China?"

"I think so. Or I'll fake it."

Deedee hummed a few bars.

"I know it in Spanish," China told them.

So Deedee sang "Turn Your Eyes upon Jesus" in English, while China sang it in Spanish. When they finished, they popped another kiss on the little ones' heads and slipped down the stairs to the living room.

Diana sat in her rocker, an afghan thrown over the back. The yellow light from the lamp cast a golden glow on her knitting. "I got a phone call from Dad," she announced.

Deedee shrugged. "Oh?"

"Our camp nurse, Trina, flew to Illinois for her sister's wedding. She'll be gone this whole week of camp."

"And?" Deedee said. "Your point is . . ."

"You and China need to know who her replacement is. Just in case someone is hurt or ill or something."

"Okay," Deedee said. "Anyone I know? Sarah from Main Camp?"

Diana shook her head, carefully maneuvering a difficult stitch. The smallest of smiles tugged at the corners of her mouth.

Deedee looked at China and rolled her eyes. "This is the old family game of 'Guess.' I never did like it. Dad adores it."

"Come on," Diana said. "It's good for you. It makes you think."

Deedee put her hands on her hips. "China, have

you noticed that if your parents want you to do something that you think is stupid, a waste of time, or ridiculous, they always say, 'It's good for you'?"

"I stay out of parent-child conflicts," China stated.

"You're a great friend," Deedee said. "Okay. Is it Marian the Librarian?"

Diana shook her head, her smile edging out further.

"Peter?"

Diana shook her head, a smile dominating her face.

"Come on, Mom. I give up."

"Doctor . . ." Diana hinted.

Deedee blanched. "You don't mean it."

Her mother nodded, looking up from her knitting. "Yep."

"China, our life is over. We thought it was bad before, but now . . ." Deedee shook her head in misery. "What are we going to do?"

CHAPTER TWO

"**W**HAT? WHO?"CHINA ASKED, looking from one to the other.

Deedee ignored her friend. "Why did Dad let him? Why couldn't someone else come? Why couldn't the 'good doctor' stay at Main Camp?"

"I'm not sure, dear. I don't question decisions like that."

"What?" China asked. "What's so awful about having a doctor here instead of a nurse?"

Deedee turned slowly to face China. "It's Doctor *Hamilton*."

China tilted her head and shrugged. "So?"

"China. Are you listening? Doctor Hamilton. Cameron Colin Hamilton the THIRD."

China stared at her friend. "I still don't get it."

Deedee turned to her mom. "Can you go senile at 15, Mom?"

"I doubt it."

Deedee put her hands on China's shoulders and

gently shook her. "Doctor Hamilton. Read my lips. Doctor Hamilton is the father of your favorite person to have for breakfast in the whole wide world."

Now it was China's turn to blanche. "Heather's dad?"

Deedee nodded bleakly.

China heard her voice grow pinched and high. "Heather's dad is going to be the doctor here this week?"

"I'm afraid so, girls," Diana said, laying down her knitting. "But don't take it so hard. It's only for one week. And at least Heather's not going to be here with him."

"Thank God for small miracles," Deedee commented.

China played with a wisp of hair. "He couldn't possibly be as bad as Heather anyway."

Deedee glared at her friend. "That shows what you know."

"Oh, come on. He's supposed to be a grown-up. An adult. Sure, they live in their own little world, wear dumb clothes and hairstyles that make no sense to us . . . but for the most part, they're like bees. You don't bother them and they buzz away harmlessly."

Mrs. Kiersey snickered.

"China," Deedee persisted, "This is *Heather's* dad. How do you think she got that way?"

China shook her head. "But at least we don't have to share a cabin with him. Be in competitions with him. We hardly ever saw Trina, so I bet we won't even see him."

Deedee slumped on the sofa, crossing her arms across her chest. "Don't count on it."

A low moan filtered through the open window. China and Deedee looked at each other and started to giggle.

"It sounds like a bear," Mrs. Kiersey said, her knitting resting motionless in her lap.

The moan came again.

"It's the boys," Deedee told her. "Last week China and I made a bear machine out of a large can and a wet shoestring."

"Explain," Mrs. Kiersey said.

"You take one of those huge cans the kitchen is so fond of . . . industrial-size food cans. Empty it. Poke a hole in the bottom. Knot a shoestring and thread it through the hole in the can. Wet the shoestring and pull your fingers down the string. The vibrations sound like a bear."

China smiled at the memory. "We scared the dickens out of the lifeguardettes."

"Shame on you!" Mrs. Kiersey said through her laughter. Her hands came back to life again, the knitting needles clicking softly.

"Then we gave the contraption to the boys," Deedee told her.

The front door flew open, the inside handle smacking the cabin wall. Adam and Joseph rushed in, their eyes wide.

"Boys!" Mrs. Kiersey said, "Quietly, please. The girls

are sleeping."

"But Mom!" protested Adam. "There's a bear out there."

Mrs. Kiersey continued to knit. "Very funny, boys. The girls told me all about it."

A bear-like noise again came floating in from somewhere outside in the darkness.

"See?" Adam said. "It really is a bear." Joseph, the quiet one, looked at his mother and nodded.

Deedee cocked her head. "Yeah, right."

"You don't see us with your stupid old machine do you?" Adam yelled at his sister.

"And you couldn't give it to a couple of your friends?" Deedee said.

Adam's face grew red. He ran down the hall and pounded up the stairs. You could hear stuff being moved. A door opening and closing. A box dragged. Then feet pounded back down the stairs. Adam stood in the hallway opening. He held up a large, tin can with a dirty shoestring dangling from the bottom.

China and Deedee looked at each other.

"Come on!" Adam persisted. "We'll show you."

Joseph nodded emphatically, his arms gesturing wildly for the girls to follow them out the door.

Deedee followed closely on the heels of her brothers. China brought up the rear. Mrs. Kiersey stood in the doorway, her knitting dangling from one hand and a strand of yarn trailing her across the floor.

Adam led the girls into the trees. The bear moaned

again, closer this time. His heavy body moved through
the brush. China could hear snufflings. Hair stood up
on the back of her neck and she shivered and per-
spired at the same time. She wished she'd brought
a flashlight. What if the boys led them too close?
Boys were known to do stuff like that. And Deedee's
brother Adam had no sense whatsoever when it came
to a potentially dangerous situation. If there was
quicksand, he'd jump in to see what it felt like.

Adam's pace slowed and he started to creep forward. Joseph turned and put his finger to his lips. All
of them tiptoed as much as possible. China's heart
pounded in her head so violently that it made her
vision seem as if it pounded, too. She was as excited
as she was scared. *To see bears up close and in the
wild! That's something to write home about!*

Adam led them into another small clearing. He
backed up to a tree and pointed into the darkness.
China stood next to Deedee trying not to make it obvious to the boys that she reached for Deedee's hand.
They linked pinkies. Deedee's hand quivered next to
China's. She breathed shallowly as they peered in the
direction Adam pointed. China tried to force her eyes
to adjust to the darkness, but she couldn't see anything. She concentrated harder, putting her whole
attention at piercing the darkness.

Deedee screamed a split second before China.
Their pinkies flew apart and China tried to run. But
the huge, furry paws clasped her shoulders so tightly

that she couldn't go anywhere. Cold, slimy stuff covered her neck and went down her T-shirt. Instantly she was surrounded by thousands of bodies. Each had a bucket and poured its contents on Deedee and China.

Gooey, smelly, pasty stuff oozed down them. One of the bodies looked an awful lot like the lifeguard called Eagle. He had massive bear paws on his hands and was trying desperately to yank them off. When he succeeded, he bent to the ground and picked up two brown guns, pointing them at the girls.

"Don't!" screamed China. "Please don't. We never meant to hurt you," she pleaded.

"So it was you!" Water Lily shrieked. "Get 'em good and stiff, boys!"

A whirring sound began all around the girls. Deedee, a lumpy figure with dark spots for eyes turned to China. "Hair dryers? How did they get hair dryers to work all the way out here?"

"Ever heard of extension cords?" Richard asked.

China knew exactly where the dryers pointed. Those spots were hot, while the other parts of her body shivered in the damp.

"Start at the top," ordered Mermaid. "Get that part good and crusty first, then tackle the bottom parts."

China wanted to open her mouth to ask what kind of goo covered them. But each time she did, some of the pasty stuff ran into her mouth.

"What," mumbled Deedee, "is all over us?"

Shark smiled, his large, white teeth gleaming in the dark. "Flour and water with a nice green food coloring mixed in."

"Why the dryers?" Deedee asked, then spat.

Shark smiled again. "That's the best part, Deedee my friend. What happens when flour and water dry? They start out a glue-like substance. But when they dry? Hard. Like plaster. We originally wanted to use plaster, but the girls talked us out of it."

"Gee, thanks," Deedee hissed.

China stared at Deedee. Her friend looked . . . well, she looked like someone covered with a green flour-and-water mixture. A lumpy, gooey live statue. China couldn't help herself. She started to laugh. She tried to keep it inside, but it just made her shake harder. Each time her laughter forced her to breathe in, she sucked in some goo off her nose, choked, tried to blow it out and laughed some more. Pretty soon, Deedee started shaking, too. Her laughs sounded more like a barking seal or a foghorn.

After 15 minutes of the dryer treatment, Bullfrog came up to China. He walked around her several times, never taking his eyes off her head. "What, pray tell, is that?"

China had forgotten about the socks. She had run out of the house with her hair all askew. Strands of hair dangled about her face with chunks still attached to the socks that fell in bizarre disarray from a purple band.

"It looks like socks," offered Richard.

Deedee snorted.

Adam poked his head into the circle. "Someone's coming!"

Instantly, all the lifeguards and lifeguardettes abandoned their artwork. China and Deedee exchanged glances. But instead of hollering for help, they stood like statues.

CHAPTER THREE

SOMETHING VERY LARGE AND CUMBERSOME plodded toward them. China felt fear run up her spine for the second time that night.

"Huh," grunted a voice. "I knew I should have brought a flashlight."

China started to snicker.

"You've been through here enough times, buddy," the voice said. "You really ought to know the way by now."

The footsteps stopped. China and Deedee crossed their fingers. They didn't want to be found ... but lacked the ability to move quickly and quietly *anywhere*.

"Hmmm. Okay. Well?" A sigh followed the sounds of someone trying to decide which way to go. "I guess I can't get too lost. I'll eventually end up in Main Camp, and then I can take the road in—like normal people."

China closed her eyes to listen better. The heavy footsteps moved forward again. She realized she was

18

holding her breath when she started to sway. She took a breath and opened her eyes just as a very large, dark form entered the clearing. His eyes grew wide and an unhuman sound came from inside his huge chest. "Uhohuhahah, AHHH!"

The girls sputtered and started laughing. The huge man quickly regained his dignity. "What are you laughing at?"

"Oh, Kemper!" Deedee said.

"Who is that? Deedee?" Kemper asked, his head tilted as he peered through the darkness at the gooey blob before him.

"And me, China."

Kemper, the high school camp director, stood in front of them, staring as if he still didn't believe what he saw. "What are you girls doing?"

"We were ambushed," Deedee said calmly.

Kemper stuck out a large finger and gently touched Deedee's arm. "What is that stuff?"

"Flour and water," Deedee told him.

"And food coloring," China added.

Kemper walked around the girls, touching them gently. "Hmm. Good idea. I hadn't thought of that one yet. I wonder how that would go over with the high school kids. What do you think?"

"*Kemper!*" Deedee said, exasperated.

Kemper shrugged. "I'm always looking for new ideas. Is there something wrong with that?"

Deedee just sighed.

"Where were you going, anyway?" China asked.

"I was actually looking for you two. But I never planned on finding you here. I wanted to ask a special favor of you. We have a new camp doctor this week..."

"So we heard," Deedee said sadly.

"... and I wondered if you two could show him around camp."

"You've got to be kidding!" Deedee said.

China added, "I thought he's been to Camp Crazy Bear a zillion times."

"He's been to Main Camp, but he's never ventured to the high school camp. I'm not sure why. I think he's always been super busy and didn't get a chance."

China wiped her mouth with the back of her green-caked hand. A few dried particles fell away. "Why us?"

"Deedee knows the camp better than anyone, and the rest of us are so busy. I also thought it might be an act of good will."

"Great," Deedee said glumly.

Kemper either didn't hear the tone of her voice or he ignored it. "Fine! I knew I could count on you girls!" He patted them both on the back, checked out his hand, rubbed it on his jeans, and marched back into the woods.

The girls looked at each other, then at the place where Kemper had disappeared. Just as China expected, after a brief moment he appeared again. "Hey. Do you guys know the way out of here?"

"Tell you what," Deedee said. "You help us get home and I'll show you the trail that leads from my house to the main trail and back to camp."

Kemper took the elbow of each girl and gave them balance to walk stiffly back home. At Deedee's house, Kemper cheerfully said good-bye and headed off toward his charges at the high school camp. Mrs. Kiersey came out of the cabin, camera in hand. "Hold still, girls!"

"Funny, Mom."

"Smile!"

China grimaced rather than smiled as the bulb flashed, the dried goop cracking on her face.

"I've brought towels out for you girls. But you must hose off that guck before you come in. It will clog up our drains, so please do a good job." Mrs. Kiersey turned on her heel and opened the creaky screen door.

"Mom—"

Mrs. Kiersey stopped.

"Did you know about this?"

"Not until the boys raced in a few minutes ago. They thought they could sneak by. But I got it out of them. Sleep well."

❧

Over an hour later the girls fell into bed, exhausted. Too soon Mrs. Kiersey came in to wake them. China pulled on her jeans cut-offs and rolled the hems. She scratched off a stray piece of green clay from her knee. "Do we have to go?"

Deedee stomped her foot into a hiking boot. "You don't. I do."

"'Whither you go, I will go' . . . and all that stuff," China quoted.

"My heart melts," Deedee quipped.

"Maybe Dr. Hamilton won't be so bad," China said.

"Don't get your hopes up," Deedee answered glumly.

"I still think we should make the best of it. Why don't we take Bologna along for company?"

The girls ate a quick breakfast of Lucky Charms, kissed the little girls on the forehead, and had three words for the boys. "Real funny, guys."

The girls headed for Rick's cabin. Rick, the assistant kitchen manager, lived across the camp in a small cabin with the little deaf dog they all shared. Since Deedee's dad was allergic to dogs, and Rick loved them, they worked out a dog-share arrangement. Once there, they snagged Bologna after saying a quick hello and promising to see Rick later in the day.

At the infirmary they found a tall, olive-skinned man rummaging through the first-aid office and nurse's quarters. With his long, slender fingers he opened drawers and slammed them shut again. "I can't believe this," he muttered. "How in the *world* do they expect me to do a good, responsible job in this place? Why this is no better than a back woods, superstitious Granny's lair."

Deedee knocked on the doorjamb. "Dr. Hamilton?"

China forced a smile as the man turned from his ransacking. His face did not register any friendliness. Yet something else had chased away the anger. "Yes? Are you ill? Hurt?" *Ah*, China thought, *the old doctor sympathy*.

"No," Deedee stated in her authoritative manner. "Remember me, Dr. Hamilton? I'm Deedee Kiersey. Dave Kiersey's daughter. I'm here to give you a tour of the camp."

"Oh, yes. Hello, Mary." His face lost the sympathetic look and took on one of tolerance.

Deedee cringed. Mary was her given name. But no one had called her that in years. Not since a young college staffer had given her the nickname D. D., short for Director's Daughter. "Please call me Deedee," she said evenly.

"Hmmh."

"This is my friend China."

China put out her hand.

Dr. Hamilton's brows went up. "I see." His hand remained at his side.

China could feel her cheeks heating up.

"We're to give you a camp tour. Shall we go?" Deedee said in her most hospitable voice. She wiggled her fingers at the deaf dog who instantly followed her. His walk was that of a drunk—a little tilted to the right and not terribly steady.

"Is the dog deaf?" Dr. Hamilton asked. "Or does he

simply have something in his ear that his owners haven't bothered to have checked?"

China chewed on her cheek while Deedee answered evenly. "He's deaf."

Deedee gave a proud shake of her head and lifted her chin. *I wish I could be like Deedee*, China thought. *She gets stronger when people are awful. I just get mad.*

With pride and confidence, Deedee led Dr. Hamilton on the general tour. Through Sweet Pea Lodge, over Grizzly Creek, by Little Bear Lake. She pointed out the boat shack, the Blob, and the battlefield, where the team competition was taking place.

During the whole tour, Dr. Hamilton nodded his head as if he knew it all already or was bored with the whole process. He frowned at the Blob and the 20-foot slide into the lake.

He should be happy with those, China thought wryly. *They could bring him more business.*

His stride was slow and even. The girls had to stop continually to wait for him. His impeccable clothing of tan slacks and a long-sleeved dress shirt with monogrammed cuffs looked out of place in these surroundings and temperature. "Does he realize he's at *camp?*" China whispered to Deedee at one point.

Deedee stretched, then pulled her flannel shirt around her. "Like daughter, like father," she replied under her breath.

At times, Dr. Hamilton whistled a low, lazy tune.

They stood on the edge of the battlefield for a few moments while teams did the bed race. Kemper sidled up to them. "What do you think of our camp, Dr. Hamilton?"

The doctor surveyed the screaming teens, sweaty bodies churning up the grass and dirt as they carried old iron beds along a specified course. He then looked at Kemper. "Actually, it makes me wonder about you."

Kemper stopped chewing his ever-present Trident fruit-flavored gum. He studied the doctor's face. "What do you mean?"

Dr. Hamilton gave a smile as honest as a used car salesman's. "I often wonder about people who work with teens. I wonder if they have something just slightly defective in their brains."

China could tell Kemper wasn't certain whether to defend himself or take this as a joke. His mouth opened several times to speak, but nothing came out. Then he took a pencil from the bushy spot of hair over one ear and jabbed it back in. The chuckle started from somewhere inside his barrel of a chest. "You're probably right," Kemper agreed. "Just ask these girls. They think I'm nuts for the games I come up with."

Dr. Hamilton stared into the distance as though he'd heard nothing Kemper had said. "Most teens are totally worthless," Dr. Hamilton stated. "They should be put away from the general population until they have the ability to behave like pleasant adults rather than overly-dramatic, pompous idiots."

China gulped. She had never wanted to hit a person so badly in her entire life. Not even Heather could compete with her dad's acid tongue. What was worse, since he was an adult and supposedly worthy of her respect, she couldn't scream at him. There was nothing, nothing she could do! Her insides knotted and puffed up until she thought she would explode. Her clenched teeth gave her an instant headache. China stared at the dirt, wishing for a moment that she was like Jesus who could write mysterious things in it and get answers.

"Cute idea, Dr. Hamilton," Kemper said lightly. China couldn't believe it. Didn't Kemper know Dr. Hamilton was *serious*? The last heat of the bed race was beginning. "I gotta run. Talk to me if you need anything." He turned and winked slyly at the girls, giving them a secret thumb's up. Some of the fury inside China dissipated. *If Kemper can overlook his rudeness, then maybe I can, too.*

Dr. Hamilton turned to the girls. "Shall we go now? I've seen enough of this outrageously moronic activity."

Deedee nodded numbly.

"Do you like toast?" China asked him suddenly.

Deedee choked back an unexpected laugh, then swallowed. "Our last stop is Eelapuash," she stated.

"Eelapuash?" Dr. Hamilton said.

"The Dining Hall. It means 'sore belly' in some Indian language."

"I bet some teen thought that one up," he said.

They walked to Eelapuash in silence. China carried Bologna some of the way to help her concentrate on something other than the stereotype of a pig-headed male in front of her. His every move was arrogant, proclaiming he was better than the rest of the world. *How dare he make fun of Kemper like that! Kemper's a better Christian than you, Dr. Hamilton.*

Dr. Hamilton turned to look at her. "It isn't very lady-like to chew on your lips, like that. A beautiful woman would never dream of such behavior," he sighed. "Beauty also has a lot to do with genes. I doubt you've had that benefit though."

China marveled at the things that could come out of his mouth. If he had said them in any other tone of voice, she could accuse him of rude behavior. But it sounded too much like a doctor just trying to help a patient.

At Eelapuash, Magda and Rick were in the throes of lunch preparations. Since John had been dismissed just the day before, they were short-handed.

Deedee's flair for making anything interesting seemed drained by Dr. Hamilton's raised chin, bored attitude, and general obnoxiousness. "This is our kitchen," she stated flatly.

Magda waddled toward them, working a towel hard to wipe the food off her hands. "Well, hello. I'm Magda, the cook." She put out her stained plump hand to shake his slender, clean one.

Dr. Hamilton kept his arms crossed at his chest and nodded his head.

After a moment of awkward silence, China spoke up. "This is Dr. Hamilton, Magda." No recognition crossed Magda's face. "Remember Heather? It's her father."

Magda's brows raised and more light came into her already happy eyes. "Pleased ta meet ya, doctor."

At that moment, Rick called from the stove at the back of the kitchen. "A doctor? Hey, Doc." In a lower tenor voice he sang, "Are you like Dr. Doolittle? Can you talk to the animals?" He let the oven door slam shut, and did a little fancy footwork—ta-DA! He threw the potholder in the air, spun around underneath it, and caught it behind his back. "I think I missed my calling," he announced as he approached the group. "I should have been a baton twirler."

Dr. Hamilton stared at him. China tried to talk to Rick with her eyes. *Please, don't, Rick. This guy will slaughter you,* she pleaded silently.

A funny look crossed Dr. Hamilton's eyes. *Evil,* thought China. *He's up to no good.*

"Maybe you should have," Dr. Hamilton told Rick dryly.

"I looked silly in a glittered tu-tu," Rick said, then laughed at his own dumb joke.

Dr. Hamilton's face didn't change. He seemed to be looking carefully at Rick's face. Then his eyes moved to Rick's shriveled arm and gaunt leg. Abruptly, he turned to Deedee. "I've seen enough. Now if you'll show me how to find my cabin from here, I would appreciate it." He nodded toward the kitchen workers. "Good day."

The warm smell of food followed them outside. Deedee led them away from Eelapuash to a trail that took them into the trees. She didn't notice that Dr. Hamilton stopped. He turned as if to examine the screen door they had let slam behind them. China, bringing up the rear, looked at him. Dr. Hamilton shook his head. "I can't believe it," he muttered.

"Believe what?" China tried to keep her anger in check, but she felt like she was trying to hold a beach ball under water.

Dr. Hamilton slipped his finger through his key ring, swinging it and catching it. He repeated the motion. Dangle, swing, catch. Dangle, swing, catch. "Where was Mr. Kiersey's head when he hired people like that?"

"What do you mean?" China asked, hearing a rumbling growl beginning at the edge of her voice.

Deedee had returned to stand behind Dr. Hamilton.

"First of all, hiring such an obese woman to cook hardly seems wise."

"Why?" asked China suppressing a hiss.

"First, her eating habits are obviously out of control. She's likely to serve the same type of diet she enjoys, which is unhealthy and fattening. Second, teens need a positive role model. And her weight is a disgrace and not in the least bit honoring to God. How are kids supposed to understand their bodies are a place where God wants to live? Is God proud of that body? I hardly think so."

China's breathing grew faster and harder.

"And that young man. I've never seen someone quite as . . . well . . . as homely as that man is. He should not be at this camp; he diminishes its reputation. Will people want to become Christians if they see someone like him around? I think not. They will wonder quite a bit about God and possibly not want to have anything to do with Him."

Behind Dr. Hamilton, Deedee looked like a dead fish with its mouth permanently open. Her green eyes stood wide and disbelieving.

China was so stunned she couldn't speak.

Dr. Hamilton sighed and moved past Deedee. "I suppose being in the high school camp it doesn't matter so much. Perhaps that's why they're here rather than somewhere else. We don't need to worry about teenagers anyway, since they're a nuisance from the age of 13 until sometime after the age of 21."

Deedee touched her finger to her lips. She shook her head, her hair swishing back and forth like a red cloud.

Dr. Hamilton turned to look at Deedee. "What are we waiting for?"

China pushed past Deedee, her eyes flashing.

Bologna, sensing her anger, barked at Dr. Hamilton.
"I'll tell you what we're waiting for," China snapped.
"We're waiting for you to be decent. To be kind to
people. To . . . to . . . stop this awful stuff you've been
saying about everybody and everything."

"Whoa, young lady. I think you need to realize to
whom you're speaking and watch your tone of voice."

"Maybe I would if you had watched your tone of
voice this morning. Who died and made you god over
everyone? Who made you the one who knows everything? I've had it with you. You put people down and
you don't even know what you're talking about."

Dr. Hamilton smiled ingratiatingly. He patted China's
head as if she were a toddler or a dog.

China ducked her head away from his touch. "Don't
touch me like I'm a puppy or a dumb kid. Because I'm
not."

"Oh?" he said, looking as if he might begin to laugh
at any moment.

"I make good decisions. I've made some good decisions while I've been here. Two good decisions—one
of which exposed your daughter's lies. All teenagers
are not awful just because your daughter is."

As soon as she said it, China wanted to stuff the
words back down her throat. But they had not only
fallen from her mouth, they had exploded in a little
cloud right in front of the doctor's face.

You'd have thought the man hadn't heard his
own daughter slammed. Nothing in his expression

changed. His eyes didn't even blink. "You've made good decisions?" he asked.

There it was again. That awful, infuriating smirk. A tentative smile that proclaimed he was superior to everyone.

China felt drained. "Yes," she said calmly.

"You had my daughter staple-gunned to a wall," he replied with the same calmness. "You left a cash box in an unsecured shack. You hid a forbidden dog." He looked at Bologna who yipped at him again. "You didn't report a broken security handle on the inside of a walk-in refrigerator." The keys jingled — dangle, swing, catch. "I don't know what 'good decisions' you could be talking about." He turned and caught Dee-dee's elbow. "Please show me to my cabin, Mary. I need to get organized before I'm needed."

Deedee walked forward, looking over her shoulder at China, her eyes large and sad.

Like a prisoner on her way to be executed, thought China. *Or worse. Like a teenager alone with a mad doctor.*

CHAPTER FOUR

THE INTENSITY OF CHINA'S ANGER DISTORTED her vision. A blood vessel pounding in her temple threatened to explode. She clenched and unclenched her fists. Then Bologna jumped at her, demanding attention. Numbly, she knelt down and scratched and petted the dog.

China stomped to her favorite thinking spot behind Eelapuash. Depositing herself on the slope of the mountain, she propped her feet on the wall. She grabbed every rock she could find and heaved them at a boulder. Smack! Crack! Bologna thought it a fun game and tried to chase the pieces of rock.

China, when are you going to stop being so stupid? When are you going to learn to keep your big mouth shut?

But I'm not sorry for what I said!

Well . . . except maybe that stuff about Heather.

Bologna trotted to her, dropping a rock in her lap. "What I said about Heather was true, you know. I just

33

shouldn't have said it to her dad." Bologna wagged his tail. "I'm glad you agree with me." She absently patted his head and threw the rock again.

The worst thing is that everything he said is true! How can you fight the truth? Magda is heavy. Rick is, to be honest, very ugly. And I, China Jasmine Tate, stumble through life making dumb mistakes.

"Bologna!" she said to the deaf dog when he returned again. She took his chin in her hand. "I've got to stop being stupid. I've got to do something really big and really positive to make up for all the dumb things I've already done. I've got to prove to Dr. Hamilton that I'm responsible and trustworthy." The little black mutt wagged his tail, then licked her face.

Seventeen rocks later, Deedee came and sat next to her. "He's a jerk," she stated.

"I can't believe he said those things!" China muttered, heaving another rock.

"Me neither."

"I'm going to prove him wrong, you know."

Deedee cleared her throat. "Is this anything like having 'sliced Heather on toast?'"

China shook her head. "No. That was mean and cruel to Heather. I've learned my lesson."

"No practical jokes on the man?"

China glared at her friend. "I'm not stupid."

"So what are you going to do?"

"I don't know yet. But it has to be something really big to prove I can do something right."

"Oh, well, you really showed him with that little display," Deedee said.

"What did you expect after what he said about Magda and Rick? Was I supposed to be sweet and calm?"

"Maybe you could have said it in a different way."

"The point is, Deedee, a stubborn mule like Dr. Hamilton is not going to be convinced that Magda is the sweetest thing that ever walked the earth. That Rick is a special person in spite of his looks. Or that all teenagers are not alien beings, unless we prove it to him."

"Oh? It's *we* now?"

"Only if you want . . ."

Deedee sighed deeply. "I'm afraid to ask. How are we going to do that?"

"I don't know yet. But my mind's spinning out of control on this one. I'm sure it won't be long before I have an answer."

"Uh-oh," Deedee said softly. "Just don't let it be illegal or stupid."

China looked at her friend. "Trust me."

"That's what I'm afraid of."

China gently slugged Deedee's arm.

⤳

That afternoon, China had a great day at work. Her decision to do something made her feel strong again. And working with Magda and Rick helped the day fly by. She didn't think about John at all. Well, maybe a little bit. At least she noticed he was gone. She hadn't realized how much tension John's anger and insecurity had caused in the kitchen. Yet now that he was gone, she felt a release. At least Dr. Hamilton didn't know about that bad decision. She never thought winning a simple arm wrestling match with John could bring out such incredible revenge. He could have killed her, and he probably wanted to.

Rick happily showed her the new security handle inside the walk-in refrigerator. He went inside with her to prove it worked. China couldn't help shaking as the door closed with a solid thud behind them. She never wanted to experience again the terror she had felt when John locked her in the walk-in on purpose. But Rick kept his hand on her arm and talked softly to her until she calmed down. He also showed her a metal rod that sat at the base of the wall next to the door. It was the exact thickness of the hole where the handle had broken off the week before. "Now we have double safety, my dear! You won't have to worry any more."

Magda bustled around the kitchen, constantly patting China's cheek and calling her China honey. "I'm so glad we're working together again, China honey! Oh, I'm so happy. My two most favorite people in the whole wide world. My Ricky and my China honey."

Rick looked at China, danced a little jig, and twirled his finger in the air around his ear. China had to keep chopping lettuce so she wouldn't burst out laughing and have to explain it to Magda.

While serving dinner to 200 crazed and starving high school kids, China had a chance to think. And watching those kids put away more food than China could imagine being consumed in one place at one time, she began to formulate a plan. A perfect plan. And it wouldn't take much. These kids would provide her with all she needed for her plan to work just right.

Deedee didn't take the same enthusiastic view of the plan. When China told her, it was as though some kind of gnat had gotten into Deedee's ear. She shook her head, her hair flying wildly. "No, China. Uh-uh. I refuse. Nope. No way. Not in a million years. Don't even think about it."

"Come on, it'll be fun!"

"Yeah, I bet that's what some guy said to his wife before they bought tickets to sail on the Titanic."

China flipped her head upside down. "I'll let you try the socks again." She peered through a veil of hair. "Please?"

Deedee took the offered brush and began to stroke madly.

"Ow!" China protested. "Not so hard."

"My dad wouldn't think it was safe."

"What isn't safe about it? We put a little garbage out, see if the real bears show up, take a couple pictures. No big deal. We don't get close to the bears. At least . . . not yet."

"Dad said we can't feed the bears."

"Did he tell you why?" China's voice sounded nasal from her upside-down position.

"No. I never questioned it. It made sense to me; it's dangerous to feed a bear."

China started to shake her head when Deedee's hand clamped down on her hair. "Don't move," Deedee reminded her.

"Deedee, why do you always accept blindly what your dad says? You need to learn to ask more questions so you know why he's saying something. Now, let's figure it out. Your dad said don't feed the bears. Why did he say that?"

Deedee's hand slowed. "Isn't it obvious? They'd bite your hand off if you tried to feed them."

"But we won't try to feed them by hand. One down. What else?"

Deedee pulled China's hair into a ponytail and wrapped it up with the purple band. "I know all the camp trash barrels are in bear-resistant containers. When they get into the garbage they make a *terrible* mess."

"We don't let them indiscriminantly rummage through the trash, Deedee. We'll put out their favorite food to snack on. I've already gone to the Nature Shack to read up on what they like. Nothing says they are harmed by human food. You know what their favorite treat is?"

Deedee shook her head.

"Melon rinds. And with the watermelon feed every week, we've got plenty to give them. But they'll eat anything. I mean *anything*. Any kind of garbage at all. Do you realize how much food some of these kids waste? We've enough to feed 20 bears." China sat on the bed and let Deedee roll her hair over the socks and tie them in a knot. She kept quiet, knowing by Deedee's clamped lips that she was thinking.

Deedee spoke in a far-off voice. "I don't know if there's any other reason why you aren't supposed to feed them. Oh, wait! I know! They keep coming back for more!" She paused for a moment, tapping the brush onto her hand. "And they lose their fear of people."

China smiled. "That's exactly it. That's what we want them to do. Keep coming back for more. We'll observe them closely and maybe even make friends with them. So what if they aren't afraid of us? We're not going to hurt them. If they lose their fear of us, then maybe we can even pet them. Or tame them just a little bit."

Deedee sat at the head of her bed, holding her pillow in her lap. She began to brush her own thick hair. "Tell me again. Why do we want to do this?"

"Two reasons. First, haven't you ever wanted to have a pet bear? They're so cute and cuddly."

"And wild and dangerous."

"But black bears aren't like grizzlies. Haven't you ever seen that old TV show, "Grizzly Adams"? This guy even has a grizzly at his beck and call. If they can do it for a TV show with a dangerous bear, I bet we could do it with a little black bear."

Deedee tossed her hairbrush toward the dresser. It fell short and clattered on the wood floor. "The second reason?"

"We prove to Dr. High and Mighty that we're not stupid teenagers. Some of us can actually do positive things and be recognized for it."

"I don't know, China. I think I should ask my dad about this one."

"It would ruin everything if someone knew before we were ready. Besides, it's too late."

"What do you mean, it's too late?"

China smiled mischievously. "That's why I was late from work. The melon rinds are in the clearing."

"You didn't."

China gave her a fake, toothy grin. "In the meantime, can we go read to Eve and Anna? They are too adorable for words."

Deedee rolled her eyes. "They're just little pains. Annoyances. You read; I'll stay here."

China adored having the two eager listeners cuddle close to her. Anna's fine hair tickled her nose and smelled faintly of watermelon. Chatty Eve kept quiet except to point out silly things in the pictures. As China tucked them in bed, listened to their sweet prayers (Anna's consisting of one word—"Bless!"), China wondered if being a mother was this wonderful all the time. Then she blushed in the darkness, remembering her hateful words to her own mother. She left the little ones, vowing to someday erase the pain in her mother's eyes she had put there.

As China quietly closed the bedroom door, she heard a noise sounding somewhat like their bear machine—but not quite. She ran down the stairs to Deedee's room. "They're here," she said, slipping on her shoes and socks.

A small bear-like sound came again.

Adam and Joseph stuck their heads into Deedee's room. "We're not falling for that again," Adam told them. "Just thought I'd let you know in case you had something 'special' planned for us."

Deedee opened her mouth to say something, but China talked right over the top of her. "Oh, nuts, Deedee. Our plan got messed up. You guys are just too smart for us." China jumped up off the bed. "I guess we'd better go tell the guys to lay off."

Deedee stared at her friend. The boys disappeared, and China shoved hiking boots into Deedee's hand. "Come on, girl! What are you waiting for? Let's go see."

The girls snagged a flashlight from a drawer in the kitchen, then slid out the side door. They tiptoed toward the clearing as snuffling, munching sounds grew louder. Once in a while, grunts of contentment mixed with the eating sounds.

China led Deedee in a zigzag fashion through the trees. "We don't want them to smell us," she reminded Deedee. She only hoped she wouldn't get them lost.

At the clearing, two brown bears with long, black-ish snouts sat pawing the ground, grabbing melon rinds and shoveling them into their mouths. Once in a while, they made small sounds to each other. Their fur glistened in the moonlight. Like her brother Cam's hair after a hard basketball workout.

China sat with her back against a tree and watched them eat, her mind whirling with possibilities. The bears were much smaller than she had imagined. She was probably taller than they were long. When they were on all fours, they came up to somewhere around her waist. About the size of a very large dog. A wolf-hound. Or mastiff. If they were that small, then it wouldn't be so difficult to train them. *I could get a collar for them. And some type of heavy leash. Wouldn't that make people go crazy to see a real bear at Little Bear Lake? We could charge 50 cents or a dollar to pet them, with all the money going to the camp. They eat garbage, so their food bill would be nothing.* The more she considered the possibilities, the more excited she got.

China tore her gaze away from the bears to look at Deedee, who sat with her legs crossed, her elbows on her thighs. Her chin rested in her hands. China tried to read Deedee's thoughts. *Good body language. She's interested. Not afraid.*

Deedee's mouth twitched. One moment she looked like she kept back a smile. *She thinks they're cute.* Then her brows would pull together and her mouth would pull down at the corners. *She's afraid of what her dad will say if he finds out.* Then her mouth pulled in a straight line and she gently shook her head. *She thinks I'm nuts.*

Deedee must have sensed China's intense stare. She turned and looked at her friend and smiled, gave a quick thumb's up, and turned her attention back to the bears.

China relaxed against the tree. She found a bunch of fresh pine needles in the dirt next to her, pulled one from the clump, and chewed on it.

The bears finished their meal. The bigger one, with the black paws, stood on his hind legs. He stuck his nose in the air and sniffed, slowly turning his body like a clumsy ballerina. He gave a short bellowed message to his buddy and the two ambled out of the clearing, straight toward China and Deedee.

CHAPTER FIVE

"**W**HAT'LL WE DO NOW?" DEEDEE ASKED frantically, her body frozen to the tree. "Climb?" Her head moved violently back and forth, looking for a climbable tree.

"No. They can climb trees," China said, trying desperately to remember what she'd read. "And we can't run, or they'll chase us."

"Great!" hissed Deedee.

"Okay, okay. Uh. Turn on the flashlight. Move it around. Don't make any noises that sound like a bear."

Deedee grabbed for the light and jumped up, stepping behind the tree.

The bears were only a few feet from them when she turned on the light.

China stood behind her tree, her heart thumping in her ears. "Cluck, cluck," she said in an even voice.

"Oh, great," Deedee said again. "Now you sound like live food."

"What do you want me to say?"

"How about, 'Go away bear'?"

"As if that would do any good."

The bigger bear lifted his head, distracted by the light and sound. The small one whimpered and turned on his heels, skedaddling back through the clearing and the bushes beyond. His sudden move must have scared the bigger one, who gave another bawl and turned to follow his brother.

"You could have had us killed!" shrieked Deedee.

"They don't eat people," insisted China, her own heart pounding.

"Yeah, right." Deedee turned toward home and stomped off into the trees, her little beam of light bouncing with every step.

China chased after her. "It wasn't so bad. We got to see them up close."

"Real fun."

"I saw your face. You thought they were cute."

"They're cute as long as they aren't after me for dessert."

"How do you know they were after us? Maybe they were just going to go down to the creek or something."

Deedee slowed. "Yeah. You're probably right. I just panicked."

The rest of the way home all they could talk about was how the bears looked. How cute they sounded. How unbelievable it was to be so close. How wonderful it all was.

❧

The next morning, Mr. Kiersey was sipping coffee at the kitchen table when the girls came downstairs. "Daddy!" Deedee said, throwing her arms around his neck.

He patted her arm and kissed her cheek. "Hi, kiddo." Then he looked at China. "Come here. While you're here, you're my daughter, too." China went over to him hesitantly. He stood up and gave her a quick hug. "No girl should be without a daddy's hug for long." He put her at arm's length. "Hey. Is your hair different?"

"Yes, Daddy," Deedee said with affectionate disgust. "Her hair is usually straight."

"Well. It's sure curly today."

China turned away so he couldn't see her blush. She stuck her head in the pantry cupboard to find the box of Cheerios.

"I rolled it in socks," Deedee said proudly.

"Socks?" Mr. Kiersey shook his head and took a sip of coffee. "Did you hear the bear last night?" he asked them.

Deedee opened the cupboard to get a couple of bowls. "I think so. Adam and Joseph thought it was the lifeguards or someone fooling around again."

"It was the real thing. Our trash container has been badly mauled. That's why I'm home. I've got to see if I can fix it. We can't have those bears in our garbage."

"They must make a real mess," China mentioned.

"They're very destructive," agreed Mr. Kiersey. He poured the rest of his coffee down the sink. "Their thoughts consist of food, food, and then, on a rare occasion—food."

The girls laughed.

"Kind of like the boys," added Deedee.

After he left, China poured herself a huge bowl of Cheerios. They floated on a sea of milk. "See? Our plan has begun to work. Already the bears know where to come for food. I didn't think it would work this fast, though."

Deedee had a tiny bit of Cheerios in the bottom of her bowl with no milk. As she ate one Cheerio at a time, she stared into her meager rations and nodded.

China swallowed a mouthful. "That means tonight they'll be back again. We'll be ready for them."

Deedee put her finger to her mouth and focused on her Cheerios. Diana Kiersey rushed into the kitchen. "Girls, I'm really sorry. But I need your help this morning. I've got a last-minute doctor's appointment. The boys can take care of themselves, but I need someone to watch the girls."

Deedee sighed with frustration. "But Mom! Why can't you take them with you? You usually do."

Mrs. Kiersey rinsed cereal bowls and placed them in the dishwasher. "Only when I don't have to go to the doctor who checks out the part of my body only the inside of my clothing sees. Sorry. It can't be helped."

China smiled. "It'll be fun, Deedee. I adore your sisters."

Deedee grimaced. "That's because you don't live with them."

"Yes, I do." China turned to Diana. "We'd be happy to watch them, Mrs. Kiersey."

"And," continued Mrs. Kiersey. "Kemper called. He desperately needs you at the mud pit."

Deedee made a face. "We really don't want to go back there."

"Sorry," Mrs. Kiersey said, taking a package of chicken legs from the freezer. "That's part of the deal with living at Crazy Bear. We help when needed."

Mrs. Kiersey paused to look at China's fluffy hair. "It's real cute, China. See you girls later."

China and Deedee re-dressed the girls in the oldest, most stained play clothes they could find. Eve could hardly contain herself. She danced and jumped and sang her own little song—"We're going to the mud pit, we're going to the mud pit."

"Mud," Anna said.

"Yes," agreed Deedee. "And we're not going to bother Kemper or the big kids are we?"

Eve stopped her song and dance, her smile turning upside down into a pout. "You said we could play in the mud."

"You can. Until the big kids come."

Deedee carried Anna on her back, pretending to be a horse, and China watched as Eve darted in and out of trees. "We're in Narnia!" Eve shouted. "And I'm Lucy!"

"Tumnus says to stay close," China told her.

The four girls went by Rick's cabin to collect Bologna. All the way to the mud pit, Eve and Bologna played tag in the trees along the side of the trail. Anna traded horsies as they tired out.

At the last curve in the trail before they reached the mud pit, China had an awful feeling come over her. Even though it was hot, she suddenly felt chilled. "Stop."

Deedee smiled. "We're not there yet. You can't play that game until we get there."

"I'm not playing," China said. She caught Eve's hand in hers and picked up Bologna. She looked at Deedee, her eyes pleading with her to understand. To see the mud pit again would be to see Bologna matted and near death.

"Why did we bring him?" China asked.

"He'll be fine," Deedee said. "He was hungry and thirsty. He's well cared for now."

China couldn't shake the feeling that something terrible was about to happen. She held onto Bologna with one arm, and Eve's hand with the other.

"Not so tight," Eve complained, her hand squirming inside China's grip.

China eased up. As they rounded the corner, the mud pit loomed before them. But again, it wasn't empty.

"What's that?" Eve asked, pointing her finger at two

large creatures wallowing in the mud. Eight furry legs waved and kicked in the air, while the two bodies writhed in the cooling happiness of mud.

Deedee stood behind her little sister and covered Eve's mouth. "Shh."

"Bears," China said quietly.

"Bearsss," Anna said even quieter.

Bologna began to squirm under China's arm.

"Why are they out?" Deedee asked. "I thought they only came out at night."

China shrugged.

"They're so cute!" Eve said. "The big one is Harold. The little one is Herman," she stated, as if she'd been introduced before.

Herman galloped through the muck to Harold, giving him a solid whack across the face. Then he turned and galloped away, Harold in hot pursuit. When Harold caught up to Herman, he jumped on top of him, pulling him down into the mud. Herman rolled over on his back and opened his mouth wide. He planted it in Harold's neck and gave a playful shake. Harold roared and jumped back. He stood on his hind legs, wobbling, checking out the situation. Herman stood on his hind legs, too, popping his head into the air with little bear chit-chat.

China tightened her grip on the struggling Bologna. When he whimpered, China held his mouth closed.

"I want one," whispered Eve. "Can we take one

home? Can we pet one? Did you bring a snack? Can I feed them?"

Deedee squatted next to her little sister. "Shh," she said into Eve's ear. "You don't want them to hear you and get scared away."

Eve nodded, putting her hand over her mouth to remind herself to keep quiet.

The brothers tumbled and rolled, mud flying everywhere. They growled and moaned at each other. They sabotaged, whacked, rolled, romped, and wallowed.

"Hey," China elbowed Deedee. "They look like us!"

Herman stood on his hind legs, his back to Harold. Harold lunged at him in a perfect tackle. Over and over they rolled. Then, as if on cue, they both stood on their hind legs, their noses probing the air. "Uh-oh," Deedee said. "They smell us."

"Maybe they're getting used to our scent," China said happily.

Deedee tilted her head, her whole face a picture of exasperation.

Bologna barked once. Then again. Then he wriggled his body and kicked out with his back legs. China let go of Eve's hand and tried to grasp the dog. But he was gone before she could grab him. His little legs covered the ground like a miniature thoroughbred. Dirt flew from his feet. High-pitched barks shot from his mouth in staccato bursts.

The bears bawled, then took off up the hillside, Bologna in hot pursuit.

"Bologna!" China yelled. "Come back here! Bologna!"

"Loaney!" Anna said.

"Bologna!" called Eve. "You get back here right this minute!"

Deedee gaped at them. "He can't hear you."

"You guys stay here," China commanded. "I'll go after him."

"Don't be stupid, China," Deedee pleaded.

"I'll be okay."

She trotted around the mud pit and followed the barks and muddy prints up the mountainside. Within 100 yards, she found Bologna running around the bottom of a tree, barking madly. She looked up into the stocky pine. One very muddy, very frightened-looking bear named Harold stared down at Bologna. Herman clung to a neighboring tree. Muddy raindrops fell around the little dog. Some landed on his head and body, but Bologna was too busy to notice.

"You stupid dog!" China called in quiet frustration. "They aren't a piece of lunch meat stuck to the ceiling. If they fall, you don't eat them, they eat you!"

China sat on the ground and stared at her dilemma. Now what? she asked herself. *What would a stupid teenager do? She would go charging over there and grab the dog or climb up in the tree after them. What would a smart teenager do? Call the dog. But how do you call a deaf dog?*

At any moment the bears could realize this tiny,

little noisy thing was more food than threat. If China chose the wrong moment to make a move, she could get hurt. Until now she'd never thought of Bologna's deafness as a problem. Now it could mean the difference between life and death.

CHAPTER SIX

CHINA REMEMBERED THE DAY she and Deedee
had discovered Bologna was deaf and how they had
accidentally gotten his attention. She stood slowly and
moved herself to a place where the bears could not
see her. Making as little sound as possible, she jumped
up and down, wildly waving her arms. She knew
Bologna's peripheral vision was excellent. Eventually
he would see her. But would he come to her?

Around and around the tree he went. Up he flew
with each bark, then back down. If he saw China's
jumping jacks, he ignored them.

Sweat began to make China's armpits slimy. Pant-
ing from exertion and heat, China picked up a rock
out of frustration and threw it near the tree.

Bologna skittered out of the way. China jumped
again. This time, the dog saw her and began running
halfway to her position, then back to the tree. Each
time he ran toward her, the bears started down the
trees. Each time he ran back, they moved back up the

54

trees. Harold, the bigger one, didn't seem to like the game. He started making swiping motions with his huge paw. Even though the paw looked clumsy and slow, China could see an immense power behind it. His playful whacks had thrown his brother face first into the mud pit. What would one blow do to Bologna? She shivered.

She shook herself from her trance, and the next time Bologna came charging toward her, she wiggled her fingers at him. Her and Deedee's intensive training paid off. Still barking, Bologna came all the way to China. She grabbed him before he had a chance to run away again.

She held him close to her chest, even though his sharp barks hurt her ears, and she walked quickly back to the mud pit, looking frequently over her shoulder.

Back at the mud pit, she handed Bologna to Deedee. "I'm too shaky to hold him one more second," she explained.

"Where are the bears?" Eve asked. "Did they chase you? Did you pet them? Are they friends with Bologna now? Are they coming back to the mud pit?"

"We hope they're on their way home by now," China told her.

"Where do they live? Where's their mom and dad? Are they big bears and married?"

China sighed. "I don't know all those answers. Why don't we play in the mud now?"

"Mud," Anna said.

"Okay!" Eve shouted, racing to the pool of slime.

"Why don't you play on the edge until we're sure the bears are gone," Deedee called to her.

The little girls squealed with delight as they stepped into the oozing mud. Anna immediately sat her padded bottom down into the murky water. She patted the surface and little gray raindrops splattered them all.

China got both girls up and held hands with them, taking them round and round in circles. "Ring around the rosy!" she sang.

Eve joined the song and Anna repeated the last word of every phrase. "Rosy!" she'd shout. "Posies!"

When they all fell down, they fell in a giggling heap. After that, they got Deedee to join them in "Row, Row, Row Your Boat." When they "stepped on the gas" they held Anna up so her feet dragged in the water as they raced around a muddy, wet circle. Bologna pranced around the edge, yapping furiously. He seemed uncertain whether someone needed his help or if the girls were only playing.

The fun for the little girls ended and work for the big girls began when the high school kids arrived. China and Deedee helped Kemper and the other staff with the mud pit games. They kept an eye on Eve and Anna who played in the dirt where they couldn't get trampled. Bologna stood guard.

Dirty, slippery team competitions of tug-of-war, steal the bacon, and spinning around with their forehead on a stick, and then trying to reach the goal

without falling headlong in the mud, filled the can-
yon with screaming teen voices. China was in charge
of watching the Locusts to make certain they followed the rules. She helped cheer them on and keep
score. Kemper put Deedee in charge of the Black
Widows.

Muddy bodies thrashed through the murky water,
slipping, falling. Kids yanked each other down, shoving and pouring mud on top of each other. In the
middle of it all, two guys stood up and faced each
other. China couldn't tell if they were just being crazy
or were mad at each other. A girl on the sidelines
screamed, "Tim!" One of the boys turned to look at
her. He gave her a silly grin. Then he turned back to
face his opponent, his chin jutting out in challenge. A
fist flew, and Tim lay flat on his back in the middle of
the water. Three staff whistles blew and the mud pit
emptied. Except for Tim. Kemper helped him up and
over to the side of the pit. For a moment, Tim was
hidden by Kemper's massive body. Then Deedee was
there, moving Tim toward the showers. She took him
by the elbow like she might a blind man.

China sprinted around the mud pit to Deedee. Tim
sucked in air and let it out in painful whimpers.

Without looking at her, Deedee said, "Go get Dr.
Hamilton. Tell him we have a possible eye injury."

China ran all the way to the nurse's office. When
she got there, she threw open the door and walked in.
"Dr. Hamilton," she said breathlessly. "We need you at

the mud pit."

When she told him what had happened, he grabbed some bottles from a cabinet and stuffed them in his bag. He looked down at his spotless clothes and sighed. "Let's go."

As they jogged back to the mud pit, China gave him more details. He shook his head and muttered something about the stupidity of high school boys. Once at the mud pit, however, he lost all sense of superiority. Instantly he became the most efficient and caring doctor China had ever seen. He gently washed out Tim's eye, talking to him in soothing yet firm tones. Tim choked back pain, sucking air through his teeth.

When Dr. Hamilton was done, he pulled China and Deedee aside. "I've got to get my Bronco and take him to the hospital. The punch drove dirt particles into his eye. I need an ultraviolet light to check out the damage. He may need some medicine the camp doesn't have. Could you girls stay with him while I go?"

They nodded.

"He can't open his eyes, so I need you to shower him off as much as possible. It wouldn't do any good to bring that stench and decay into the emergency room."

In that moment, he looked around. "Whoever let those two little girls around this bacteria pit are irresponsible fools. If the high school kids want to rot their bodies, that's their problem. But they should protect the little innocent ones."

"Kemper puts chlorine in the pit before they use it," China said defensively.

Dr. Hamilton didn't seem to hear. Already he was striding quickly down the trail.

Deedee and China shoved Tim underneath the icy spray of the outdoor shower and gave him instructions on where stubborn clumps of muck clung to him so that he could wash it off. As he finished, Dr. Hamilton returned. In a flash, the doctor wrapped Tim in towels, put him in the Bronco, and drove off.

With the competition over, Deedee showered with Anna, and China showered with Eve. "Did you see what happened, China?" Eve chattered. "I wish I saw. But I didn't. Did he hit him hard? That was so much fun. Can I do it again? Can we come back tomorrow?" Suddenly China felt tired. She tuned out Eve's chatter and hoped she didn't ignore something important.

As she held Eve's hand on the way back to the house, she could only wonder if she had put these two precious girls in danger. Was it wrong to take them to the pit? She and Deedee hadn't gotten sick when they played there. She tightened her grip on the little girl's hand and smiled down at her. She never wanted to hurt these little girls. Never. She couldn't live with herself if she did.

"I like you, China," Eve said to her. "When I can read better, I'll read you *Green Eggs and Ham.*"

"I'd like that," China said to her, the warmth in her heart spreading into her smile.

Back at the house they all showered again; this time with soap and warm water. China took a quick nap before lunch with Bologna curled up next to her. She woke remembering all the things Dr. Hamilton had said to her. She didn't like them because they were true. And if they were true, then it meant she was more than just a klutz. It meant she would be better off if she curled up somewhere permanently so that no one could be bothered by her presence. *So I won't think about that. I've got more fun things to worry about—like how we're going to tame those bears.*

After lunch, Deedee went to the boat shack and China went to the kitchen. Magda met her with worry scrunching her brow. "China honey. I need you to scrub 100 pounds of potatoes, then lay them on trays for baking."

She turned and moved away, huffing as if she'd climbed a mountain.

"Magda," China said, running up behind her. "What's wrong? You look so upset."

"Nothing to matter your mind over, honey."

China ran around her and put her hands on her hips. "Tell me."

A hand behind her landed on her head and mussed up her hair. China jumped and twirled around. "Rick! You bum! You scared me!"

"I'd say I'm sorry, but I'm not."

"Gee. What a friend," China told him.

Magda moved away, clattering pots and pans as she unhooked them from the overhead rack and took them with her. When she was out of earshot, China whispered to Rick. "What's wrong with Magda?"

"Someone tried to break into the kitchen last night," he whispered back.

"Do they know who?"

Rick shook his head.

"Should we worry?"

"Magda's worrying enough for all of us. Probably just some kids looking for a midnight snack."

CHAPTER SEVEN

THE WARM SMELLS OF THE CAMP KITCHEN enveloped her like a quilt. Inside the kitchen she felt safe. Here she could be herself. Here she could burst into a crazy song and not be laughed at . . . and Rick would probably join in. Magda's face would beam with joy as she moved about the kitchen, her hands full of ingredients to make something good to eat. In the kitchen China always worked hard and felt satisfied with herself. She felt like she was accomplishing something worthwhile.

At home in Guatemala, she tended to wander around, figuratively running into walls. She felt crabby and without energy. Doing chores at home stifled her and made her insides feel knotted up with anger and frustration. The same chores here made her feel light, wanted, needed, and helpful.

Scrubbing a zillion dirty potatoes could have been an ugly, boring chore. But China pretended they were all brown baby bears who'd stayed too long in the mud pit and then lay in the sun to dry. They needed tender scrubbing. *I won't hurt you, little bears. I will clean you up and help you to feel safe, so you don't have to run and hide in trees.*

Occasionally she would burst into song. "Whistle while you work!" she sang out at the top of her lungs. And an answering whistle came from wherever Rick was.

Rick rarely stood still. He was always on the move —opening ovens, mixing batter, cutting huge hunks of beef, stirring beans, while Magda seasoned.

Nothing satisfied China more than this warm place of food and love. The only thing that would make it perfect would be to have Deedee and Bologna here with her.

She placed the potatoes on large cooking trays and Rick began to bustle around her now, picking up trays and moving them to ovens. "Did you stab them first?" he asked.

"Oh, wait." She cringed as she stabbed her bear babies, having to tell herself they were only potatoes and didn't feel a thing.

As Rick waited, he leaned against the sink watching her carefully. "How come you like practical jokes so much, China?"

She jabbed without looking at him. "I love to see people laugh. I love to see people in unexpected situations. It's not much fun when they don't see things the way you do, though. I try to be careful about who

I play with."

"You didn't take my yogurt joke too well," he reminded her. "Should I not play jokes any more? You're not one of those people who can dish it out but can't take it, are you?"

Now China looked at him, her eyes round and pleading. "Oh, please don't stop any jokes. I really do love them. I just didn't know who you were at first. Having someone play jokes to be mean is not fun at all."

"I wasn't trying to be mean."

"I know that now. I know you're my friend."

His eager nod and smile brought the kitchen warmth even closer.

"I did hear of an incredible joke though. You're not going to believe this one, China," Rick said.

"Try me." China kept stabbing potatoes, feeling like her hand might fall off at the wrist.

"These guys beat your practical jokes by a mile."

"So tell me. Maybe I can use the idea."

"You won't want to."

"I always love a new joke," China said. "There, finished," she put down the fork and started to scrub more potatoes.

"Okay. Remember, you asked for this. The guys in cabin Night Hawk went back to change after lunch and discovered the inside of their cabin looked more like the great outdoors. Someone had covered the floor in dirt, made mounds and transplanted trees, and had used some sort of foil turkey roasting pan to make a lake. To top it off, they even made a mud pit complete with mud and little people in the mud."

"Whoa! Verrry clever. But I don't think I'd do that."

"I told you."

"That could be so destructive to the cabin. And the kids. Are they furious?"

"Actually, they're not upset at all. They get to sleep outside tonight because it's going to take maintenance a long time to thoroughly clean out the mess. They also have to disinfect the place. So the guys get to sleep under the stars."

China handed him a tray. "Yeah, they'll love that."

Rick disappeared with the tray, then returned moments later for another one. China scrubbed, poked, and dropped her final potatoes on trays. Magda mysteriously showed up the moment the last potato hit the tray. "Time to brown the ground beef." She took China by the hand and patted it. "I hope you don't mind me holding your hand, China honey. But sometimes it's the only physical touch Magda gets. And I'm a hugger from way back. It's tough when there's no one in life to touch you."

China patted Magda back. "I don't mind at all. I actually like it." China quickly looked down at the floor, not wanting Magda to read her eyes. If Magda could see inside her, she would know China ached to be touched. To be hugged. To have someone want to be with her. Every time she looked at a magazine, there were always couples with huge smiles hugging, holding hands, somehow touching.

"Well, then," Magda said, "we'll have to be touchers together then. Rick's a toucher too. That's why he's always grabbin' one of us to dance."

As the raw meat sizzled, China chopped and stirred to break it up into little pieces. Magda stood next to her, tending to the beans. "Magda," China asked, "how do you survive in this place?"

"Whatever do you mean, China honey?"

"I mean, no one knows who you are. Without you, there'd be no camp. And yet the only kids who know you exist are the ones with KP duty."

Magda chuckled. "Yep. I've often wondered at them kids eatin' like there's no tomorrow. Maybe they think food generates itself in here." She chuckled again. "No, China. My work is for my Lord. I work to please Him. I know He wants me to cook my best and keep learnin' how to cook better. I don't need recognition. I've got all I need."

China chopped and stirred, thinking about living a life where no one ever knew she worked hard. Where the people who benefited most from her hard efforts didn't appreciate it. "I think I'd want to be noticed. You know, at least some kind of thank-you at the end of the week."

"Makes no matter to me, China honey. I love all them kids. That's why I'm here. I asked for this job. It didn't ask for me. I wouldn't trade my place to be the most well-known chef in the world."

The sizzle disappeared; a soft bubbling now cooked the meat. "Okay. But what if someone marched in here and told you that who and what you were wasn't good enough. That you really had no place on this earth. What if they made fun of your decision to have the potato bar and chili? Or any of your other menus." China wanted so badly to rat on Dr. Hamilton. To tell Magda what an awful, rude person he was.

"I can't build who I am on what other people think, China honey. If I did, I'd march off the closest cliff. Because I'm sure there's plenty of folks out there who'd think that best just 'cuz I'm heavy."

"So what are you supposed to base who you are on? How are you supposed to know if you're a good person? How do you know you should stick around this earth?"

Magda stopped seasoning the beans and stared at China. "You ain't thinkin' of suicide, are you girl?"

"Oh, no, Magda. It's just that sometimes people are so mean. They say such awful things."

"Don't believe them."

"But Magda," China felt a wail in her voice. "The things he said are true."

Magda heaved a huge sigh. She nodded. "I know, honey. The truth hurts more than anything. But you still can't look at what they say as a definition of who you are."

"Then what do you do? How do you define who you are?"

"I have to understand who I am from God's perspective. If I can understand that, it don't make no difference what another person thinks." Magda tasted her beans and nodded with satisfaction. She placed the spoon in the sterilizing solution next to the sink.

"But this person acts like I should be perfect. He also expects me to not be a teenager. How can I stop being what I am? It's like asking him to stop being a 40-something-year-old."

"We're all growing. All learning. I love that verse in one of the Johns that says we're to practice righteousness. Makes me think of practicin' the piano. We ain't got it yet, but we're still practicin'. We won't get it right this side of eternity . . . but one day we'll get it right." Magda's eyes rolled, and her hands came up to clasp her heart. "And oh! what a day that will be for me."

Magda turned China around and pulled her close. China melted into the softness that was Magda. "China honey. You just keep lookin' to Jesus. You just keep knowin' you're already a saint. Just because you don't got it perfect yet doesn't mean you aren't one. Just keep doing what's best, the best you can."

When Magda released her, China felt whole and loved. Just like that. Just like she was. With no additions. No changes.

She turned the heat off from underneath the meat and snagged Rick to hold the strainer while she poured the grease off. Rick winked at her. "I don't know what she told you," he said in a whisper. "But don't forget it.

She's got you glowing. It makes you prettier than you already are."

China blushed. Catching herself, she put her chin up in the air. "You're not coming on to me, are you Mister Rick? We can't have fraternizing of the help, you know."

Rick chucked her under the chin. "Accept a compliment, girl." He turned and walked away.

China stared after him and pondered everything she'd heard.

CHAPTER EIGHT

ALL EVENING CHINA PRACTICED her right-eousness. She practiced doing what was right. When one kid came in to complain that his potato was undercooked, instead of saying, "So what do you expect me to do about it?" she apologized for the inconvenience and gave him one she knew was done. When Dr. Hamilton came in to complain that his strict low-fat diet would be ruined by the meal, China quietly gathered some extra vegetables and low-fat cheese for him. Afterward, Magda came up and gave her a sideways squeeze. "You did just fine."

During clean-up, Deedee came to help. "I've got to tell you what happened this afternoon," Deedee told her as she unloaded dishes. "One of the cabins . . ."

"I already heard," China told her.

"Well?" Deedee said, holding her yellow-gloved hands up in the air. "Doesn't that give you any ideas?"

China smiled. "Is it supposed to?"

"Oh, come on, China!" Deedee flipped her hair

around. "You know it does."

"Well, actually Rick had a fun idea. It's not really a joke, but it would still be fun." China explained the plan.

Deedee pouted. "Well, that's okay. But I would have preferred a joke."

"You won't like my second idea either." China shoved another tray of dirty dishes into the dishwasher and slammed the metal doors closed. She wiped her brow with the back of her arm.

"What? More bears?" asked Deedee.

"That too. But I want to go to the meeting tonight."

Deedee stacked the dry plastic dishes and slid them onto the cart. China could see that she didn't want to go. They'd discussed this so many times.

Deedee tried to drape some of her thick hair behind her ear. It stuck to her rubber glove instead. "Okay, I guess there's really nothing else to do tonight anyway. Besides, if we're going to stay over here on this side of camp for our little plan, then it might be something to pass the time."

After they finished the dishes, they dropped their used aprons into a laundry bag. Once inside Sweet Pea Lodge, they slid onto the cold metal folding chairs with the usual "oohs" as the chill touched their bare legs. China knew Deedee would be okay by the time the Fong brothers hit their second praise song. She joined right in rockin' out and singing with gusto like the rest of them.

Kemper sauntered up and bonked them both gently on the head. "Hey, you two," he said with a giant smile.

After the songs, Kemper called kids up from each team to play a game for points. "It's called IRON GUT," he bellowed without a microphone. "So only those of you who think you have an iron gut need apply. One team member from each group of insects scurry on down, right now!"

The lodge filled with shouts and encouragements. Eventually, five bodies appeared up front.

Kenisha, one of the staff members, played the part of a game-show bimbo. She stood behind a draped table. Her slender black hands indicated the table in front of her, a perfect, fake smile on her lips.

Kemper bounced around, enthusiasm leading him around the stage. "LADIES AND GENTLEMEN," he announced, "WE ARE ABOUT TO DISCOVER WHO THE TRUE IRON GUT IS. KENISHA? PLEASE REMOVE THE CLOTH."

With a flourish, the red-and-white checkered cloth fluttered in the air and disappeared behind the table. On it stood two rows of boxes. The front row had 10 numbered small boxes. The elevated rear row had five numbered large boxes.

"Uh-oh, look." China pointed to Rick who appeared from behind the stage, blender in hand. "I wondered what mischief he was up to. He was wandering all over the kitchen being so nosy. And Magda ignored him."

"My friend Rick, here," Kemper boomed, "is our happy chef."

Rick wore a tall, white chef's hat and sported a clean apron. He grinned at the audience and bowed. China marveled that he never seemed to know or care that his looks would never win him a beauty contest.

"Contestant number one. From the Black Widows." Kemper motioned for a stocky Asian boy to come closer. "You will choose two boxes from the lower level and one from the upper level. Rick will make you a luscious shake from those ingredients, which you will hold until the others have a chance to get their shakes."

The Black Widow chose boxes one and five, and box three. Kenisha tossed the boxes behind her and they crashed on the stage. She daintily picked up the items one at a time to hand them to Kemper. "Ahh! Your shake will consist of chocolate pudding, green beans, and maple syrup!"

The whole audience moaned. "That's gross!" called a voice.

Kemper turned to them and smiled. "Why do you think we call this Iron Gut?"

One of the contestants ran back to his seat. "Come back here!" Kemper called. After a brief, noisy huddle, another from his team trotted to the front.

The Locusts got lucky with yogurt, apple crisp, and milk. The Tarantulas picked sardines, granola, and prune juice. Tomatoes, peaches, and chocolate syrup went into the Scorpion team's cup. And olives, salsa, and chunky buttermilk made a yummy shake for the Stink Bugs.

China felt green just watching them.

"Before you begin, I want to show you THE SPEW BUCKET! This little item is here in case what you put in must come out! Are you ready? ON THE COUNT OF THREE." As Kemper counted, Kenisha kept her fake smile and held the spew bucket.

"THREE!"

Supporting team members screamed and shouted as those who felt they could chug anything gulped down their shakes. Deedee sat with wide eyes, one hand to her mouth, the other to her stomach. China kept muttering, "Oh, this is so sick." She'd watch, then she'd turn away, afraid the bucket would be put to use.

A blond representing the Stink Bugs jumped up and down, her cup empty.

"Don't jump," China begged from her chair. "Oh, please don't jump."

Kemper raised her hand high as she wiped the liquid from her upper lip.

As the contestants trooped back to their places, China shuddered. "I'm glad my week as a camper is over. He seems to be coming up with grosser stuff all the time."

Deedee nodded. "Scary thing is, they love it."

China, looking around the turbulent room, had to agree.

The Fong brothers led three more songs. The first one was fast, the next two progressively quieter. China leaned to Deedee. "There's a real method to this madness, isn't there?"

Kemper popped on stage again. Without his Bible. China looked at Deedee, questions in her eyes. Kemper never talked seriously to the kids without his Bible. Deedee shrugged.

"I'm so excited," Kemper said.

"He's always excited," Deedee offered.

"Tonight we have a special guest. None of the other kids this summer are going to get this privilege. I decided you guys could live without me for most of the evening. So I've asked Dr. Hamilton, famous trauma surgeon, to speak to you."

China sank in her chair. She looked around, hoping for a way of escape. But this must not be a 1 Corinthians 10:13 moment. There was no way of escape. Her eyes pleaded with Deedee.

"This was your idea," Deedee hissed in response.

China sighed and crossed her arms across her chest as Dr. Hamilton walked straight and poised to the stage. To some, the smile he gave might have seemed genuine. But China thought it was totally fake.

Kemper shook Dr. Hamilton's hand, then asked, "What does your job consist of, Dr. Hamilton?"

"Most of the time, I clean up messes other people make through foolish decisions."

China flashed Deedee an ugly look. "What is it with

this man and dumb decisions?"

Deedee leaned and whispered in her ear. "Maybe it's because he's never made any."

Kemper's brows pulled together. "I'm not sure I follow you."

Dr. Hamilton's slender hands moved in slow, steady, surgical movements as he talked. "Much of what I deal with comes from automobile accidents—most involving alcohol or drugs. Then there are stab and gunshot wounds from fights. Necks broken from shallow dives or motorcycle accidents." Dr. Hamilton looked out across the sea of kids, then directly into Kemper's eyes. "I would be out of a job if people, especially teenagers, made better decisions."

"I imagine your job involves decisions, also, Doctor."

"A trauma surgeon must judge the worst injury at the moment and attack that first. He's like a soldier in the war against bacteria, illness, pain, and death. Sometimes he even has to choose which part of a person he will let die. For example, choosing to repair the heart means the kidneys will die or be so damaged that the patient will be on dialysis for the rest of his life. The most difficult decision comes when you must decide when to quit trying to save a patient. When to quit trying to keep them alive. There's a fine line in knowing when revival of a person would be more damaging than letting him die."

China felt funny inside. She couldn't imagine

making those kinds of decisions. She hadn't realized anyone would ever have to do something like deciding death over life.

Kemper had the mike again. "Doctor, how does this affect your walk with God?"

The closest thing to emotion China had yet seen crossed Dr. Hamilton's body. His perfect posture drooped imperceptibly. But only for a moment. In an instant, he was self-controlled again, his words measured and perfect. "It is a humbling thing to 'play God.' But I would never want God's role. Just think; every day He must decide who receives mercy. Who receives justice. Who lives, who dies." Dr. Hamilton shook his head in awe. "My job gives me more respect for God and a kind of camaraderie with Him. At least God has the advantage of being all-knowing. I guess I see God as someone so enormous, I don't even hesitate to give my life to Him."

Kemper stood silent a moment, then asked a little more hesitantly. "You mentioned the difficulty in making decisions about when to quit medical assistance. Have you ever made a decision you've regretted?"

Uh-oh, here comes the atomic blast. China leaned forward, putting the palms of her hands on the cold chair.

Dr. Hamilton again searched the room. China was grateful he didn't seem to see her. He cleared his throat. "I wish I could say I've never made a mistake. But there have been times when I don't know if I've made the right decision."

China gulped.

"And," he paused and looked down at his hands, "there are some wrong decisions I've had to learn to live with and accept."

China thought she'd fall flat on the floor. Or her eyes would fall out and roll until they bumped into the stage. *He's admitting to making wrong decisions? He who puts me down so drastically about my own decisions?*

"What is the most important quality someone must have to do your job?" asked Kemper.

Deedee leaned into China's ear. "It sounds like career day at camp."

China nodded.

Dr. Hamilton seemed to stand even straighter, his chin level, eyes piercing, his manner commanding. "The most important quality I must have is a kind of superiority."

A bunch of murmurs traveled about the room.

Kemper gave him a funny look. "I don't think I understand."

"I must have respect and authority. To command that, I must appear to all my coworkers as someone superior to them. Superior in knowledge and understanding of a situation. I must be obeyed immediately and without question."

China leaned over to Deedee. "You're right. He's a jerk!"

Deedee nodded. "Wonder no more where Heather got it."

"If I do not remain somewhat aloof—if I become buddy-buddy with anyone in the trauma center—then they may begin to doubt my decisions. In trauma situations, even 30 seconds of doubt can mean life or death.

"If I do not give the appearance of knowing precisely what I'm doing, my coworkers would begin to lose their trust in me. If even one nurse, one arm of the surgery team, or one family member of the victim does not immediately trust my authority and obey or respond instantly, someone could die needlessly. Or they could have a more permanent injury than necessary."

"Thank you, Dr. Hamilton," Kemper said, shaking his hand again, and sending him on his way.

Kemper trotted off the stage and grabbed his Bible. He returned to his place and opened the Bible. "It seems to me that so often we, as Christians, must obey God without knowing why. We must act without hesitation. Or someone could die . . . literally or spiritually. If we don't obey Him, we could find ourselves in a situation where the consequences could affect us or someone else for the rest of our lives."

China stared at Kemper, looked at Deedee in unbelief, and back at Kemper again. *How can he do that? How can he tie everything up with something true about God?* Inside China's imaginative mind flashed scenarios that showed how it all tied together. That obedience sometimes must come even though you don't why. She promised God she'd try to remember this one. That she'd try to obey Him even if she didn't understand why.

CHAPTER NINE

AFTER THE MEETING, China and Deedee went out a side door of Sweet Pea Lodge and walked a few feet into the trees. Without talking, they sat in the semi-darkness, alone with their thoughts. After a few moments, China spoke in a quiet voice. "What do you make of it?"

Deedee moved her hair behind her ears. "It's one of those things like a puzzle piece from the wrong puzzle. It's too big. Its cuts are different. And you don't know how to make it fit."

China nodded. "It makes you think."

"Just when I thought I had him in the proper place..."

"Jerk," China offered.

"...yeah...he pops out and I have to start all over again."

"Maybe he plays the superior role in intensive situations so much that he doesn't know how to be normal."

Deedee thought a moment, then nodded almost

imperceptibly. "You might be right."

"But I still don't think that gives him an excuse to be rude."

"Me neither."

Something small and close to the ground came scurrying toward the girls. They froze for a moment, their attention in the direction of the sound.

"Bologna!" cried Deedee.

"Where'd you come from, little guy?" China asked him.

The little dog raced from one girl to the other, swiping both with an eager pink tongue.

Momentarily, a much larger creature came huffing up the path. "Hey, you two," Rick said, limping toward them. He plopped on the ground between them. "I thought we had a plan."

Bologna made his rounds over and over, then found a stick to drop in China's lap. She threw it for him. He ran, compensating for his eastward list, fetched, then dropped it in Deedee's lap.

"We haven't forgotten the plan," Deedee told him, checking her watch. "I didn't think we needed to be there quite yet."

"What?" he said, pretending to be horrified. "You expect me to make the preparations all by myself?"

China stood, dusting off her seat. "Course not. Here we are, at your service."

The three trudged through the trees toward the kitchen. Bologna followed, the stick still in his mouth.

Rick used his set of keys to let them into the kitchen. China remembered her plan to try to obey God. "Did you get Magda's permission?" she asked.

"Of course. She made us promise to only use the items on our list and to clean up the kitchen. I, on the other hand, am totally responsible to make sure it is locked up tight. We don't want anyone breaking in."

Before they got down to serious work, they felt obligated to give Bologna a snack. From the ceiling, of course. Deedee heaved an American cheese triangle to the ceiling. Bologna began to do his little jig, barking and hopping, staring at the ceiling. Rick looked at the dog a moment, then began dancing a jig of his own, yapping at the ceiling like the dog. The poor dog didn't know what to make of this big person dancing around beside him. He yapped at the stuck cheese, then yapped at Rick, then sat his little behind on the floor and cocked his head. His floppy-tipped ears perked up and he sat and watched the crazy person.

China held her aching sides and howled with laughter. Deedee honked. Both had tears pouring down their faces.

The cheese never did unglue itself from the ceiling. Rick had to stand on a rolling table, steadied by the girls, and attack it with a long-handled barbecue spatula.

After the cheese disappeared into Bologna's eager mouth, a silly grin took over his whole face. "One more try," he announced.

"Oh, no!" the girls groaned.

Rick disappeared into the walk-in and reappeared with two half-moons of bologna. The lunch meat quickly cooperated . . . sticking to the ceiling, then falling into Bologna's mouth after a time. After the dog munched the second piece of lunch meat, Rick gave them all tasks.

While the girls made peanut butter and jelly sandwiches, Rick danced around the kitchen, gathering napkins and a couple of checkered tablecloths. He disappeared into the walk-in freezer, returning with some bags of broken cookies. He had China make a cooler full of grape punch. As she mixed the concentrate in a garbage can used only for making punch, Rick excused himself, taking the dog with him to his cabin. When he returned, he wore black pants and a white shirt. Over that he had on a crisp, clean apron, his collapsed chef's hat underneath one arm. While he was gone, the girls had dressed in black skirts and white blouses, crisp aprons covering their clothes also. They put their hair up into tight buns with white bows perched on top.

The three friends stepped into the cool night. The pines smelled even stronger at night, their fragrance like a joy drug to China's heart. She looked at Rick, who carried the heavy cooler of punch. His chinless profile no longer made her shiver with disgust. On the other side of Rick, Deedee carried the tablecloths and tubes of plastic cups. China held the cloth bag with the cookies and sandwiches. Nothing could rob her of the contentment she felt. She could do this for the rest of her life—live in the mountains, serve others.

Wordlessly they moved through the trees and chaparral, the moon spraying silver across their path. Some of the silver spattered the sky like glitter. *God, is this what heaven is like?*

A sly smile crossed Rick's face. "There's something I didn't tell you," he whispered.

Deedee's eyes narrowed. "What? Are we going to get blasted again?"

Rick shook his head, his smile taking over his whole face. "Right now, the counselor is telling them a scary story. He's getting them all worked up. Then, at the scariest point in the story, I ring my bell and totally scare them to death."

"Cool," China said, thinking how delicious it is to be scared when it's safe.

Deedee shook her head. "You guys are so mean."

"Oh, Deeds. You know you love it," China said.

"The story isn't a bad one," Rick assured her. "It isn't about ghosts or witches or anything evil. Actually, the kids in the story have imaginations that are over active. Just because the butler acts strange and they can't see their grandmother, they get all bent out of shape."

"Do you know the story?" China asked, a shiver prickling her arms.

"A little. The basic idea. But the counselor goes into real detail. He's such a good storyteller. You could swear you're right there when he tells it."

"Well, tell us anyway," Deedee begged.

"Two teenagers, a boy and a girl, are sent to live with their grandmother after the death of their parents. The stone house is old and stands alone, away from other houses at the top of a windswept hill. When they arrive, Harris the butler answers the door. In his hand, he carries a knife, which frightens the kids. He is emotionless, proper, and attempts to hide the knife discreetly behind his back."

"If he didn't do anything wrong, why did he hide the knife?" Deedee asked, tossing her head out of habit, as if to get the curls out of her face.

"He's a butler. He's also the cook, as the grandmother can't afford to hire one anymore. So, he had been slicing meat in the kitchen when the doorbell rang. But being a proper bulter, he couldn't let the guests see the stained knife."

"But the storyteller doesn't mention that part," China said.

"Of course not." Rick put his load down, stretched his arms, then picked it back up again. "When they ask to see their grandmother, the butler tells them she is ill and does not wish to be disturbed. When the kids try to use the phone, they find it has been shut off. They feel like prisoners in the house, forbidden to go into the dark, dank east wing, from which a horrible stench is filtering through. The butler has an extra-sensitive ability to hear. So the kids cannot move anywhere without the butler knowing where they are and what they are doing.

"They figure their poor grandmother must be dead, killed by the butler. And they know they are going to be next. They talk over their options and decide to escape at midnight." The group moved around a boulder, up a hill. Rick put his finger to his lips. "This is where we come in," he whispered.

Through the trees, the displaced boys from cabin Night Hawk sat in rapt attention to the storyteller. Never had China seen a group of boys so still and quiet.

Rick put the cooler down, fluffed up his hat, and placed it carefully on his head. From his shirt pocket he removed a gold dinner bell and white gloves. He motioned for Deedee to pull out the tablecloths. China quickly set out the sandwiches and cookies on a tray. The girls positioned themselves as dignified guards of the food.

The storyteller's voice moved through the words, giving them life. China felt shiver follow shiver as she looked at the butler through the eyes of two imaginative kids.

"One summer evening," the storyteller said, "when the moon was bright and silver, just as it is tonight," (some of the boys looked up at the moon) ". . . the kids snuck downstairs. This was the night they would make their escape. They had to get past the butler. As they moved past the kitchen, the lights went out, and they were in the pitch-black darkness. Everywhere they moved, scuffling shoes followed. With their hair standing up on the back of their necks, and their hearts pounding in their chests, they bolted. All of a sudden..."

Right on cue, Rick rang his dinner bell, the clapper beating wildly on the bronze metal. Every boy sat bolt upright, some gasping, a few yelling. Then all heads turned toward the frantic ringing. A lone voice said quietly, "It's the butler."

Rick bowed, then said formally, "Your feast is served."

China tried to compose herself. Even in the short time she had listened, she'd gotten caught up in the story. She did not expect the raucous bell shattering the night. She mentally shook herself and stood, poised as the butler's helper.

No one moved. China had to force herself not to smile as some of the boys moved slowly away from them. Fear widened their eyes.

Rick again bowed low. "Do not be afraid," he said formally. "Your grandmother will be joining us for breakfast. Her fever has broken and she is finally able to keep food down. She encouraged us to celebrate with this midnight feast."

Someone started laughing, his laughter igniting the others. They all stood, shoving each other, punching each other, each one swearing they had not been afraid.

"This is so fabulous," one guy said, plopping himself down on the dirt. "A midnight feast."

"Not exactly midnight," said another voice, "but who cares."

Rick silently motioned the boys to sit around the cloths. The girls poured drinks and served them.

"You guys are great!"

Mostly the servers smiled and nodded. "At your service." "Would you care for more beverage?" Their formal actions and words transformed the rowdy bunch into snickering gentlemen. Sometimes China had a tough time keeping a straight face.

When the food had disappeared, the boys from Night Hawk cabin slipped away to their sleeping bags. They sat, talking about what made them afraid. How their own imaginations can sometimes make them see things differently than they really are. And how God fit into it all. And who He might be. Like the butler? Not always giving answers, but expecting trust and obedience? And how some people think He's mean. And others who think He's just there to wait on them hand and foot like a butler. And others who weren't so sure who God was.

Rick produced a plastic garbage bag, and all three scoured the area for litter. Deedee folded the tablecloths and China tied off the garbage bag. The chef's hat and gloves disappeared. They walked back into the night as they had come. Only this time with their own thoughts swirling inside their heads, keeping them quiet.

The spell didn't really break until they reached Eel-apuash.

Rick spoke first. "Hey. Something's not right."

"You didn't plan your own scary story for us, did you?" China said.

"You guys can be so suspicious," Rick said, looking a little hurt. "I'm not going to mess with you. We're on the same team, okay?"

The girls nodded. Rick moved toward the door, as if he were a cop being careful of an ambush. He approached the door from off to one side, rather than directly. It was then China noticed that the screen door seemed shredded. It hung open at an angle. "Do you think..."

"You guys stay here," Rick whispered. "I'll go check it out." He set the cooler down, placing the hat, gloves, and bell on top. Cautiously, he moved toward the door.

China put down the bag of trash, Deedee, the table-cloths, and she reached for China's hand. Both girls stared at the door as Rick moved inside.

China moved slowly toward the door, pulling Dee-dee behind her. She tried to peer into the dark kitchen, but could see nothing. A pungent odor seemed to come from inside the kitchen. Her brain tried to connect the odor with something but couldn't come up with anything. But the smell made her skin crawl.

Rick made no sound. But something else did. The sound of someone bumping into a shelf in the darkness. Cans crashing.

"Hey! You!" Rick shouted suddenly, flicking on a light. "What d'you think . . ." Then, his voice changed. It became full of sounds and feelings. "Oh, no, uh-oh, Oh, no!"

The girls ran to the door and opened it, charging inside. China grabbed an oversized spatula for barbecues, and Deedee grabbed a fork. Rick came tearing around the corner, his face white. "Go! Run! Come on!"

China watched him without comprehension. Thoughts sped through her mind. *Someone has a gun. Why would someone have a gun in a kitchen? A knife? Why would they be after Rick? I'm not going anywhere. It has to be a joke. No one would hurt us here in Camp Crazy Bear.*

He moved past them, trying to grab at them as he ran. The crashing behind him continued. Moments later mutters and grunts, definitely not human, mingled with recent memories. China looked at Deedee. At the same instant, they mouthed the word "BEARS."

Before they could turn and follow Rick, two ghostly apparitions came charging through the kitchen. Amber fluid dripped from their fur, dotting the floor. A white powder covered them from head to toe. One of the bears sneezed and shook his head violently as he ran. The other ran a couple steps, paused to lick his sticky leg, then ran again. He seemed undecided whether he should run or stop and snack. His little brother seemed to make up his mind for him. And the two smashed through the screen door.

China and Deedee stood as sentries, their weapons still poised in the air. Stunned, China stepped over to an amber spot on the floor. She stuck her finger in it and smelled it. Then, not believing her sense of smell, she tasted it. A quizzical look crossed her face. Then she bent over and tasted the powder. "Flour," she stated matter-of-factly. She tasted the amber liquid again. "And *syrup?*"

Then it erupted. Deedee started it. And China didn't hesitate to join in. The laugh started with a little giggle and grew into gales of guffaws and tears pouring down their faces. Rick's face appeared in the ruined screen door. "You guys okay?"

That started their laughter all over again. China laughed until her stomach hurt, and she couldn't stop laughing even then.

"We could have gotten killed!" Rick said, stepping through the screen door without bothering to open it.

Deedee shook her head, unable to stop laughing long enough to talk.

"Sure, go ahead and laugh," Rick said, pouting. He grabbed the barbecue utensils from the girls and hung them back up.

"What?" China said through her tears. "I can see the headlines now, 'Kitchen Workers Killed by Two Gummy Bears.'"

That sent the girls into fresh laughter. Deedee
laughed so hard she honked, which made China laugh
even harder. Rick tried to keep himself from laughing,
but it didn't last long. Pretty soon he was howling
louder than the girls.

It took them some time to settle down, at which
point Rick called Security to report what had happened. He maintained his professional attitude until
he snickered, snorted, then hooted that the damage
had been done by a couple of gummy bears.

A long pause on the other end of the phone line.
Then, "Is this some kind of joke?"

"No, sir," Rick said, trying to stifle his laughter.

"You are trying to make me believe little pieces of
candy broke into the kitchen?"

Rick howled, trying to tell the girls what Security
had thought. China rolled into a ball on the ground
holding her stomach, tears pouring down her face.
Deedee honked some more.

"No," Rick finally managed to get out. "Bears. Real
bears. Covered with syrup and flour."

When he hung up, he turned to the girls. "Security
doesn't find this quite as funny as we do. We're not to
clean it up until they check it out. I don't think they
believe me."

Deedee stared at him. "Gee, Rick. I wonder why not!"

Security showed up within 10 minutes of the call.
They flashed their lights on the door, inspected the
torn screen, smelled the drops of fluid on the floor

and checked out the mess in the back. "It's bear all right," the chief Security officer said, writing officiously on a clipboard. "Did you let the bears in?" he asked without looking up.

Rick looked at the girls with a "Can you believe this idiot?" glance. The girls looked at the officer and gave him forced, sick grins.

His radio crackled at his belt. "Excuse me one minute." He turned up the dial on his radio.

"1089 alert. 1089 with 1522 immediately. Near cabin Night Hawk."

The Security officer blanched. He spoke into the radio. "Are you sure?"

"Ten-four."

The Security officer fastened the radio to his belt. "I've got to run. Those bears you saw have moved on to new territory. The Night Hawk boys have reported a bear injury."

China, Deedee, and Rick stared after the men as they opened the ruined screen door and ran off into the darkness.

CHAPTER TEN

"**L**ET'S FOLLOW THEM," Rick said, ripping off his apron.

The girls ripped off theirs, letting them lie where they dropped. Rick closed the broken door, no longer worried some human might break in.

The three ran back over the same route they'd taken just a half hour before. China's heart pounded in her chest, both from exertion and adrenalin, her feet pounding the forest floor. She sucked in the night air. It stung her teeth with its coolness.

They arrived in the middle of absolute chaos. Some boys had dragged their bags into the trees. Some laughed and shouted as they relayed the incident over and over again. The gospel of the bear visit according to Sam, Mike, Johnny, and Chris. Others gestured wildly at the Security team, their voices coming all at once. The volume escalated as each one tried to talk over the other.

China felt any laughter squelched by the possibility

that someone, somewhere was hurt. She scanned the boys, looking for someone on the ground or clutching a part of their body as blood leaked out. But she saw nothing.

"Calm down," the Security officer tried to say over the din. "CALM DOWN!"

No one listened.

Deedee put her fingers to her mouth and whistled. Instantly all eyes turned in her direction. She smiled weakly and dropped her hand to her side.

The Security officer took advantage of the silence, by saying, "Okay, everyone, sit down! Is anyone hurt?"

Two boys raised their hands. The Security officer waved them over. He looked at their hands and one foot. He motioned China and Deedee over. "Take them to the doctor," he told them. Then, in a whisper, "I don't think they're really hurt. But better have the doctor check them out anyway."

"So," Deedee said, letting her hair free from the confining bun. "Tell us what happened."

China pulled a few bobbie pins from her hair and let it fall freely to her shoulders.

"Well," said the kid named José, "we had all decided to be real quiet and look at the stars. One of those dumb games where the first person to make a noise loses."

Kirk spoke up. "Then we heard something like someone walking in giant slippers."

José shoved his hand through his hair. "I figured it

was boys from another cabin, coming to try to scare us. Or part of the counselor's story—like you guys were."

"Me, too," added Kirk. "I held real still, thinking if these guys thought we were asleep, they might come close, then I could grab one and give him a good yank. He'd end up on his nose. I slipped my hands out of my bag to be ready for them. My palms up, like an open trap."

José started talking faster. "I didn't think of that. But I held real still. And then I heard real heavy breathing. And then everything happened so fast. All the guys closer to the sound stayed real still, even though I knew the cabin trying to scare us would have to be right on top of them."

Kirk continued the story. "I smelled this horrible smell with kind of a syrupy whiff along the edges. Something licked my hand. I pulled it away and these sharp teeth almost grabbed me. I reached up to grab this stupid kid's nose and yank it off. But I got a handful of animal hair instead."

José nodded frantically. "Kirk screamed and I sat up. Just as I did, this huge white thing pounced on my bag and ripped it to smithereens. I bopped the thing hard on his head and he took off running."

Kirk shook his head. "It was so strange. They were all covered in syrup and something else."

"Flour," Deedee offered.

"You know about this?" José asked.

"They broke into the kitchen," China told them.

"Here's the doctor," Deedee said, coming up to a dark cabin. She knocked tentatively on the door. "Dr. Hamilton?" she called. "We have two possible bear injuries for you."

They left the boys with the doctor before he could blame them. Returning to the kitchen, they met Rick, who sat on the preparation table, broom in hand, staring toward the pantry.

Deedee grabbed a huge wooden spoon, then stood with her hands on her hips. She clucked a little, sounding much like Magda. Then she waved her wooden spoon at him. "Why haven't you started cleaning up, Rick? Can't you do anything without us?"

Rick barely glanced at her, then returned to staring. "I've been sitting here trying to figure out what I should do next. I didn't know where to start."

Deedee surveyed the pantry area. Her jaw dropped. She crossed her arms and tapped the spoon in the air.

"What's with you guys?" China asked. "It's not that bad, is it?" She rounded the corner to the pantry and stared. The pantry was actually a narrow hallway lined with shelves. Every shelf except one had fallen or had been broken. Canned goods, broken jars, spices, odd pottery dishes, plastic storage containers, buckets of flours, pasta, beans, and rice had all fallen into the hallway. "It looks like we just had an earthquake."

"A bear quake," Deedee said solemnly.

Rick suddenly snapped out of his trance. He jumped up and clapped his hands together. "I've got it! In *Mary Poppins* she got the kids to do work by singing a great song."

Deedee lowered her chin and looked at him as though he'd lost his mind.

China immediately knew what he was up to. "A Spoonful of Sugar!"

Rick grabbed her hands and they spun around the room singing at the top of their lungs until they had the whole song whistling through the air, filling the room with fun rather than depressing frustration. Pretty soon the bulky items littering the pantry floor stood upright on the preparation table. Deedee hummed and sang as she plunged a sponge into a bucket of soapy water and washed the syrup off the floor and walls. China swept away the flour, rice, and beans that had escaped their storage units. Rick replaced the unbroken shelves. They were still singing when Magda found them.

"Who tore my screen apart?" She demanded as she marched into the kitchen. When she saw the three of them hard at work, she didn't even wait for a reply to her first question. "What are you doing at midnight? You're going to an awful lot of work for a snack."

Rick smiled like a little kid caught doing something he wasn't sure was okay. "We already did that."

"Then what? Spring cleaning? In the middle of the night? And who ruined my screen?"

Rick put his arm around Magda. "You did have someone break in tonight."

Magda stood up straighter, her eyes flashing. She tried to pull away from Rick's grip. "Who? Who would dare break into Magda's kitchen?" At that moment she saw the broken shelves. "And WHO would dare break my shelves? I'll break his little slimy neck!"

China tried to keep a straight face. She'd never seen Magda so angry.

"I don't think you want to mess with who did this damage, Magda," Rick said, his face drawn up into a parental, instructional mode.

"Hah! You think I'm scared? They mess with Magda's kitchen, and they mess with a She Bear."

Rick flashed a toothless smile. "That's close."

Deedee came to Magda's rescue. "Two bears came in here, Magda."

Magda's anger bubble popped. Deflated, she wasn't sure what to say or believe. She looked at China for verification.

"We caught them. They really wanted food, I guess. They found the syrup bucket and clawed a hole in it. After it doused them, we came in and scared them. Well, actually Rick did."

Magda turned to look at Rick. "I can understand that. Rick would scare anybody."

Rick gave her a playful pinch on the arm.

Deedee squeezed out her sponge. "They made a real mess. So we're cleaning it up."

Magda walked over and kissed Deedee's forehead. "Thank you." Then she kissed China's forehead. When she got to Rick, he blushed and moved quickly away, humming "Hello Dolly" under his breath.

Magda made notes of the damage on a lined yellow pad of paper. The whole time, she wished out loud that the fellows on the construction crew were on 24-hour call.

After she left for bed, still mumbling under her breath, Rick insisted on walking the girls back to Deedee's cabin. "We don't need a chaperon," Deedee protested.

China chuckled. "As if Rick could stop a hungry bear from taking a swipe at us."

Rick stood taller. "I could let him take a swipe at me while you got away."

"Awww, isn't that sweet?" Deedee said, her face taking on a kind of marshmallow look.

China rolled her eyes. "Nice try, Rick."

"What?" He said looking from the face of adoration to the one of mere tolerance. "What did I do?"

Rick made them stomp and slam bushes with sticks in order to keep away any flour-covered bears who might want a second helping. China did her stomping and slamming half-heartedly. *How am I supposed to make friends with these furry little guys if they're scared of me?*

Rick was so intent on his beating process, he didn't even notice.

After the girls said their good-byes, they could hear Rick noisily making his retreat through the forest.

Before their heads hit the pillow, they decided it was time to step up their plan. These hungry bears needed available food, or they might break into the kitchen again. "Tomorrow night," Deedee promised in a sleepy voice.

"Mmm" was all China had to say.

CHAPTER ELEVEN

CHINA WOKE DEEDEE THE NEXT MORNING.
"Deedee. Your mom says we have to take the boys
with us to the battlefield this morning."

Deedee groaned and rolled over. She pulled her
pillow over her head. "It's too early."

"It's 9:00. You can make it. I know you can. I have
faith in you."

"The boys know where the battlefield is," Deedee
replied. "They can get their on their own."

China sat on the edge of the bed and bounced,
bobbing Deedee off the surface with each bounce.
"Your mom wants to make sure they hear what goes
on at the special meeting."

"What special meeting?" Deedee said from under
her pillow.

"A ranger is coming to talk about bear safety. Your
mom wants the boys to hear this and not ditch it."
China pulled the pillow off Deedee's head and
whopped her with it. "Now."

Deedee squinted against the daylight. "I hate you, China Jasmine Tate. I do. I really do."

China smiled. "Of course you do. Now GET UP!"

Deedee lifted herself onto one elbow. "'Blah,' said Toad."

Within half an hour, China and Deedee herded two sulking boys to the battlefield.

"We don't need a baby-sitter," Adam complained.

Joseph shook his head in sad, slow agreement.

"Why do we have to go to this stupid thing anyway?" Adam said, kicking a rock.

Joseph looked at his sister.

Deedee put on a face that looked just like her mother's. "You have to go to this 'stupid thing' because Mom said you do."

Adam kicked the rock again. "So? We can ditch." Joseph nodded his assent, looking hopefully at Deedee.

"No, we can't," Deedee told him. "Mom said it, so we do it."

"But *why?*" Adam pestered.

"I don't know. Because she's Mom."

"That doesn't tell me why. I want to know why."

Deedee looked at China and rolled her eyes. China came to Deedee's rescue. "Sometimes adults want us to be safe, so they tell us to do things that will help us be safe."

"But I know how to be safe around a bear," Adam insisted.

"So humor her and listen anyway," China encouraged. "Besides, maybe the ranger will tell some interesting stories."

That seemed to perk up Adam and Joseph. They even elbowed everyone to get a front-row seat on the grass.

A ranger had set up portable panels on which he'd put various taxidermied wild animals. A long table sat in front of the panel with a few larger animals whose faces were eternally frozen in a petrified snarl. China recognized only a few of them: a red fox, a great horned owl, a woodpecker, a chipmunk, a blue jay, a shrew, a mouse, a rat, and a bobcat. The others were familiar creatures but not ones she had names for. A rope barrier kept the kids far from the exhibit.

China and Deedee sat in the back so they could lie down and sunbathe if the ranger got too boring. Both had worn bathing suits under their shirts so they could take the greatest advantage of the summer sun.

The high school kids in front of them grew impatient waiting for the lecture to begin. A group at one side began the wave. Pretty soon the whole group performed it. Then the teams started chanting their cheers. It wasn't until the ranger blew a whistle that a sense of order returned to the battlefield.

"We've had some unusual bear incidents in the past two days," the ranger began. "Your camp director, Mr. Kiersey, decided it was important for you to have some instructions on bear safety in case you should encounter these bears.

"First of all, it's unusual for bears to travel in pairs. Most often they are loners. This leads us to believe these two fellas are cubs who were abandoned by their mother at a young age."

A sad chorus of female voices rose from the group. "Ohhh."

"Because they are young," the ranger continued, "they don't know the proper manners or ways of hunting."

A voice called out from the crowd. "We heard someone got their hand bit off last night by a huge, white bear."

The ranger smiled. "A group of campers had eaten peanut butter and jelly sandwiches and hadn't washed their hands afterwards. The bears simply came along and licked what smelled good. No one was bit. Only a small bit of blood was drawn when the boy yanked his hand out of the bear's mouth." He paused to chuckle. "The white bear was actually a California black bear covered with flour he'd managed to dump on himself in the kitchen."

The crowd laughed.

China raised her hand. After the ranger called on her, she said, "You called them black bears. But the ones we saw were brown."

The ranger chuckled. "Since when did we Americans start making sense?"

The crowd laughed.

The ranger continued. "California black bears can be black, brown, cinnamon, or even shades of yellow or blue." He shrugged his shoulders. "Why? I don't know."

A small hand down in front shot up into the air. Deedee groaned.

Adam's voice could be heard all the way in back. "Do you have some funny stories to tell?"

The ranger nodded. "Bears are very smart creatures. They have almost human intelligence. They've been known to turn on sprinklers at a golf course to cool off when it is hot. Some have climbed in windows and sat at tables to dine on cake, cookies, and silver polish. One person came home to find a bear going through his refrigerator. When it comes to food, these guys will do anything to get it. Although they are smart, their stomachs rule their brains."

"Kind of like the high school guys," a girl's voice shot out from the crowd.

"OOO, OOO, OOO," hooted others.

The ranger lifted his hand, waiting for quiet before he continued. "Because of this, every camper must be sure not to take food into his or her cabin, and you must make sure to wash your hands frequently . . . especially before bed. Although these bears are cute and smart and can be lots of fun to watch, they are still wild animals. Generally they are docile creatures and afraid of people. But that doesn't mean they are not extremely dangerous. The more comfortable they become in an area, the more they will guard what they consider to be their territory."

The ranger stepped around the table, walking closer to the crowd. "As you hike the trails here in Camp Crazy Bear, there are several things to do for bear safety. First of all, walk noisily. Bears don't like surprises. And you're never sure if they will attack or run away. So be sure to make a lot of noise."

"Yeah," someone shouted. "Make sure to take Kemper with you everywhere you go." Everyone laughed. Kemper playfully tossed a wadded-up paper in the direction of the voice.

"If you can't take Kemper," the ranger continued, "just be sure to make noise. If a bear approaches you, do not run."

"Should we climb a tree?"

"No. These bears have curved claws and can climb trees easier than you and I. Stay calm. Back away slowly. But never run. Then you become game. If you cannot back away, be very quiet and still. Black bears are not known to attack people. But we don't want to take any chances."

As he talked, a crashing noise came from behind him. To everyone's total amazement, the two bears, with some flour still hidden in their fur, charged toward them. The ranger held up his arms in a gesture for everyone to remain quiet and seated. Then he sank quietly to the ground, turning to face the bears.

The bears galloped toward the display, grunting and moaning as if the group wasn't there. China would have thought the campers were invisible, but Harold turned, looked at the group, and turned away, as if he didn't care that he had an audience. He went straight for the bobcat and sank his teeth into the furry back. He chomped down on it, then stood back, almost in surprise. He swayed back and forth on his hind legs, looking curiously at the animal that didn't bleed. He munched, then seemed to not care the animal was abnormal. Herman launched his attack on the paneled smaller critters. He used his paw to pull the animals from the panel then shovel them into his mouth.

In a flash, taxidermied fur and guts of glass, shredded wood, and bits of clay wire flew about in the bears' feasting frenzy. China wondered that none of the girls were freaking out. Some looked totally stunned. Others held a hand over their mouths. A soft voice in front of her said, "They're so cute!"

After the first glance in their direction, the bears seemed oblivious to the presence of 200 kids. All they wanted was food. Fake food. Deedee leaned over to her. "I thought bears were supposed to be smart."

Harold popped a field mouse into his mouth, then wandered off after Herman who had already tired of the strange-tasting food.

Even after the bears were gone, everyone stared at the destruction in silence. Even the ranger. Then he seemed to wake and compose himself. "Now, that was a lesson, wasn't it! You see, as I said, bears are more interested in food than anything else. But never forget these are wild animals, and *all* wild animals are potentially dangerous. Have a great day, and keep safe."

China whispered to Deedee. "Those poor fellows must be awfully hungry if they're willing to eat stuffed animals like that. We need to make sure they get more food."

Deedee looked at her friend skeptically.

"If we feed them, they'll leave the kitchen and other kids alone."

"I don't know, China."

The crowd of kids dispersed, most moving toward the area where the bears had destroyed the animals. Adam and Joseph wove in and out of the high school kids at top speed. "Wasn't that cool, Deedee?" Adam asked, his voice breathless from excitement as much as from the physical exertion of running. His hands moved wildly. "Man, oh, man, I've never seen anything so cool. It would have been even better if the animals had been alive."

"Adam!"

Joseph quivered with excitement. He pointed toward the destroyed exhibit. "That was totally awesome," he said, pronouncing each word separately as if each were its own sentence.

China stared at him, then at Deedee. "He talks!"

Deedee looked her brothers over. "I guess it must have been amazing."

"Do we have to stay here? Or with you?" Adam asked, unable to keep still.

Deedee shrugged. "I guess you can go. Mom only wanted to make sure you heard the talk."

"C'mon, Joseph! Let's find the bears." In a flash, they were gone in the direction of the bears.

China watched them go, arms pumping speed into their gait. "A lot of good that talk did for them."

Deedee shaded her eyes against the bright sun. "Do you think they'll find them?"

"I doubt it."

CHAPTER TWELVE

IT WAS TOO HOT TO SLEEP IN THE HOUSE.
Even with all the windows open, the air hung heavy
and still. "Who sent the heat wave?" China asked.

Deedee wiped her forehead with the corner of her
sleeveless flannel shirt. She put down her Scrabble
tiles to spell Bologna. "Twelve points."

Like silent cherubs, Eve and Anna appeared in the
doorway holding hands. As soon as China looked up
at them, Anna raced into her lap. "Hot," she said.

Eve cautiously approached her sister. "Deedee.
Where's Mama? We can't sleep."

Anna nodded. "Hot," she said again, then buried
her face in China's neck.

Deedee stroked the damp hair from Eve's face.
"Mama and Daddy went on a litle trip down to the
valley overnight."

"Can you call her? Tell her to come home?" Eve's
eyes filled with tears.

"They aren't very far away, but Mama said not to

112

call unless it's an emergency. We'll be okay."

"But I'm so hot."

"I don't know what to do, honey. Maybe we could spread a sheet down out here."

Eve shook her head. "It's too hot out here, too."

China studied her Scrabble tiles, trying to figure out what she could do with the overabundance of vowels in front of her.

"Could we sleep outside?" Eve asked.

Deedee shook her head. "I don't think so. You're too little. What if Anna got up and wandered away in the night?"

China looked up from her tiles. "You and I could sleep outside with them."

Deedee stared at her tiles. It seemed she ignored China. After shuffling the tiles, she sighed and chose another. "I suppose we could. Should we worry about the bears?"

"I don't think so," China assured her. "The ranger says they really don't like people. And we put enough garbage in the clearing to make sure they get enough food for the night. They'll eat and go home."

Deedee spoke without looking up from her tiles. "We'd better wash the girls' hands, The ranger said the bears last night were attracted to the peanut butter on the boys' hands."

"We could sleep down by the creek," China suggested. *That's far enough away from the clearing that we won't even hear them,* she thought.

"I wish Mom was here. She always knows what to do when it's hot."

"Has she ever let you sleep outside before?" China asked.

"All the time. She feels it's real safe up here."

China laid out her tiles. Boo was all she could spell with so little to choose from. "Five points." She smoothed Anna's hair and kissed the top of her head. At barely two, the baby smell still clung to her skin. Her hair smelled like a freshly sliced watermelon. Anna sucked her thumb furiously. China tried not to think about the rising temperature with two hot bodies so close together. Instead she closed her eyes and drank in the wonderful smell of watermelon and baby.

"We'll have to take the boys with us," Deedee said. "They are a total pain." She slid new tiles onto the game board. "Fifteen points."

"I heard your mom tell Adam he'll have to have a baby-sitter stay with him everywhere he goes for a week if he doesn't obey you."

Deedee sighed. "Okay, fine."

China whispered to Anna, "Can you get a blanket and come back down here?"

Anna nodded. She climbed down from China's lap. "Doggie?"

China shook her head, "No, we won't bring Bologna."

Anna ran away. She returned carrying a stuffed

dog. "Doggie?"

China smiled. "Yes, you can bring your doggie."

Deedee gathered sleeping bags to lay on the ground for padding, while China gathered sheets and pillows. The boys punched each other and whooped and hollered. "Hey!" Deedee said in a stern voice. "Chill down."

"Who do you think you are?" Adam commanded.

China answered. "She's your boss, captain, general, pilot, and head cowboy."

Adam kicked the ground. "Fine," he said with reluctant resignation.

The troops headed out into the hot night air. The sun left streaks of golden amber across the sky. Deedee led, while China took up the rear, carrying Anna. China watched the boys, thinking of her own little brother, Nic, still in Guatemala. Adam and Joseph didn't bug her as much as they bugged Deedee. They weren't such bad kids. Obnoxious sometimes. But not bad. *Maybe Nic isn't so bad either. I wonder what Deedee would think of Nic. She'd probably think he's adorable. Everyone else does.*

The sky grew darker, the sound of the creek closer. Suddenly, China ached for her family. She ached to see Cam with his nose tied to an invisible string that moved it from side to side—from textbook to term paper to textbook to dictionary to thesaurus. She tried to see him through Deedee's eyes and blushed. She'd probably think he's cute, too. She shook her head as if to make the puzzle picture fall into place. Cam, cute? Deedee would make China's mom and dad laugh with her hair flipping from side to side, her funny expressions, and subtle humor. She wished she could get them together somehow.

China shifted Anna from one arm to the other. The walk made Anna's head heavy with sleep. Pretty soon, her breathing was soft, slow, and even.

Being away from her family made China see them a little differently. But not different enough to want to go back. She never wanted to go back to Guatemala.

At the creek, Deedee made the boys clear the ground of large rocks. They didn't mind the task, hucking each rock into the creek. When they were done, Deedee unzipped the sleeping bags, laying them out on the ground. China found a boulder and sat on it with the sleeping Anna weighing heavy in her arms.

When the beds were finished, China and Deedee lay down on the outside of the huge bed with the little girls between them. Deedee let the boys set up their camp a little ways away from them.

The creek cooled the hot air to a comfortable temperature. The rolling sound soothed China to sleep.

In her dreams, bears unzipped their heavy fur, stepping out of it like a coat. Underneath they wore candy-striped pajamas. They tiptoed up to China's bed at Deedee's house and climbed in, curling up with a doggie stuffed animal.

At times she slept deeply. At other times she felt

she was barely under the blanket of sleep. And then, the rush of water became distant and everything went black and silent.

↝

Horrible, piercing screams split China's darkness into a black-gray light. Screams mingled with rushing water. China bolted upright, her hair brushing something large and heavy. She flipped over on her hands and knees. Anna's screams connected with her conscious mind. A large, wet, black nose hovered over Anna's head. Massive jaws clamped down on a soft baby head. China didn't think. She jumped to her feet and screamed something ancient. Something animal. Furious. She clasped her hands together, raised them over her head, and with all the power she ever had, she brought them down as a sledge hammer on the bear's ugly head.

Startled, the bear released his prey and moaned his protest. China raised her fists again and came down harder on his sensitive nose. The bear bellowed and took off running. His little brother galloped to keep up.

China panted, her hands still clutching each other, unable to let go. She watched the bears disappear. Slowly her ears lost their deafness. They opened to the screams of Eve, the hysterical cries of pain from Anna, and Deedee making sounds and moving about, trying to have purpose to her actions, but not succeeding.

Adam and Joseph rushed over. They stood, bare-foot, eyes wide, saying nothing.

Blood poured from Anna's head. China didn't want to look but knew she must. Deedee hovered over Eve, trying to calm her down. She touched Eve everywhere trying to find out if she screamed from pain or fear. "Calm down, sweetie," she said over and over in a quivering voice. "Calm down."

China couldn't talk. She felt a bursting dam of tears inside her chest. She bit her lip as she lowered herself to Anna who raised her arms to be picked up. But China couldn't do that. Not yet. She had to find out what to do. What it was. How bad.

She swallowed hard to swallow back her own fear. Her tears. Her panic. She stretched a violently shak-ing hand toward the massive river of blood running down Anna's head and soaking into her pillow. She touched Anna's head and did not feel hair. She felt something soft yet hard. Then she saw it. A flap of skin peeled back.

"Take her," Deedee said. "Take her and run. Run to the doctor. She's losing too much blood."

Without hesitating, China scooped up the little bundle and grabbed the folded pillowcase Deedee shoved at her. She put the pillowcase on top of Anna's head and began to run. The rocks tore at her feet. *Please don't die, baby. Please don't die.*

A small person ran alongside her. Joseph. His round eyes looked hopefully at her. Pleaded with her. She knew what they said. *You can do it, China. I believe in you. I trust you.*

China felt tears pouring down her face. They trusted her. And she hurt them. They trusted her. What could she have done? How did this happen? Black bears don't bite people.

She pulled Anna closer. Little Bear Lake came into view. Slid by them. Past Eelapuash. Past Sweet Pea. Only a few more feet.

She pounded on the cabin door. "Dr. Hamilton! DR. HAMILTON!" Joseph's fists pounded with hers.

"What is it?" came the sleepy voice inside.

"It's China. We have a horrible bear wound."

A moan. "Like last time, China? Go away."

China choked in unbelief. "He doesn't believe me!" she wailed to Joseph.

"Why should I? You're the queen of pranksters," Dr. Hamilton said. "Now, good night."

China pounded on the door, her voice filled with shrieking panic. "Open the door, Dr. Hamilton! Please!"

From inside she heard a horrible sound. A scoff. Then a shift in bed. China looked at Joseph, then at the bloody bundle in her arms. She stared at the door. *What am I going to do?*

CHAPTER THIRTEEN

OUT OF EXTREME FRUSTRATION CHINA kicked at the door. Joseph simply grabbed the handle and opened it. Dr. Hamilton shot out of bed. "You two . . ." His voice stopped when he saw the blood. "Bring the baby here. What's her name?"

"Anna."

Dr. Hamilton moved the blood-soaked pillowcase briefly. "Hi, Anna." China had never heard such a calm, sweet, loving voice. "You're okay, sweetheart."

He turned his head away from the little girl. "Joseph. Run to the infirmary and bring me anything that even looks remotely like medicine. China. Get my black bag from over there on the chair. Then get me a pan of warm water. And a cloth."

China did as she was told. Anna's whimpers of fear turned to silence. Her eyes opened wide. She watched every move the doctor made.

Dr. Hamilton lay the baby on the bed. Without looking at China, he gave quick commands. "Open my bag. Inside you will find some sterile, sealed packages. Hand me the suture needle. Also the suture thread."

The items were easy to find. Dr. Hamilton's bag was laid out so neatly. Not like any purse China had ever seen.

Dr. Hamilton's hands moved quickly. He threaded the large needle with the black thread that looked an awful lot like fishing line. He grasped the needle with some kind of forceps. The only sound was the needle driver clicking on and off as it locked its jaws onto the needle, drove it into the edges of the wound, then unlocked to pull it through the other side.

"I thought you had to wash a wound first," China said quietly, her voice a soft question, not an accusation.

Dr. Hamilton paused only a split moment to look at her face, judging something he saw there. He turned back to his work. "I've seen people bleed to death from scalp wounds. The only way to stop the bleeding is to stitch it. Immediately. We'll cleanse it later. Then give her an antibiotic. But it's more important to save the patient's life than have a clean wound."

China's knees decided to stop being bone and turn into squishy stuff that couldn't bear her weight. *Bleed to death? Save the patient?* She sat down on the floor. *Oh, dear God. Please don't let Anna die.* Her thoughts tormented her. *What would it be like if Anna died? Where would they bury her? What would Mrs. Kiersey do? What would Eve do?* She pictured a tiny casket flooded with flowers. Everyone crying. No one ever speaking to her again. She shook away the morbid pictures. But then, if this is what they all had to look forward to, wouldn't she be better off if she was prepared? The truth would be better than not knowing. "How bad is it?" China finally whispered.

"I don't know for sure yet. She will need a transfusion."

Joseph walked in with a box of clanking bottles. "I brought shot things, too."

"Good boy," the doctor said without looking up from his work. "Find the bottle that says 'Betadine.' Give it to China. She'll mix some with warm water to look like weak tea. Then get me an injection kit and a bottle of penicillin if you have any."

While China and Joseph followed instructions, Mr. and Mrs. Kiersey burst through the door. Mrs. Kiersey trembled, her hands reaching for Anna, then folding back to her heart. China's tears ran for her. What must it be like to be a mother and see your precious baby like this?

Mr. Kiersey hugged China. "You can go home now."

"No," she said in a whisper, her focus still on Anna. "I can't."

Mr. Kiersey stood with his arm around China. She could feel his fear through his hold on her. He had little strength left, she could tell.

Dr. Hamilton finished whipping careful, tiny stitches

around Anna's head. There was so much blood that China couldn't see the blond wispy hair at all.

The doctor took the solution China had made, as well as a clean cloth. He dribbled the liquid around the wound, then peered closely. "I think we have the bleeding almost stopped."

China waited. She waited for Anna to sit up. To cry. To reach for her mom. Her dad. China. To suck her thumb. Ask for her doggie. Something. Anything.

Anna did nothing.

"The danger is not over," Dr. Hamilton said frankly, yet his voice was calm and reassuring. "Scalp wounds can be quite dangerous. She has lost quite a bit of blood and needs a transfusion. Also, she needs antibiotics to fight infection. No matter what, she needs to be under constant care for the next couple days."

Mrs. Kiersey nodded as she stroked Anna's arm, watching her child's face.

Dr. Hamilton wrapped a quilt around the baby and gently scooped her into his arms. "Mr. Kiersey, will you drive?"

Mr. Kiersey started out the door, then stopped. "My car is back at the house."

"Drive mine." Dr. Hamilton nodded toward the table where a ring of keys lay.

China stood behind Joseph, her hands resting on his shoulders. The entourage passed them without a word. Then Mr. Kiersey turned back. "China. Take care of my family while I'm gone."

When the car disappeared, the dam of tears inside China finally burst. After the first rushing sobs consumed her, she choked them back, closing the hole in the dam.

China marched forward like a soldier who has seen combat and didn't expect it to be like that. The whole way home she held Joseph's trembling hand in hers. At the house, she told Joseph and Adam to climb in bed. She held Eve, who screamed and screamed. With every creak of the house Eve thought she heard bears. Numbly, China could only rock her, petting her hair until the screams turned to sobs that turned to tears and then to exhausted sleep.

Still numb, China talked to Deedee like a robot programmed for words, not emotions. The robot heard Deedee's anger that she had had to stay with the other kids and couldn't be with her own baby sister. But everything that happened to China happened at arm's length. As if she watched a movie rather than participated in the events.

She lay in bed for the final few hours before sunrise. She didn't sleep. She didn't close her eyes. She stared at nothing.

China didn't truly realize the day had passed until she finished washing the dishes in the camp kitchen. She took off her apron and wondered what she'd done that day. Had she talked with Rick? Had she played with Bologna? What had Magda said to her? She couldn't remember.

Back at Deedee's house, she sat in the living room and listened to the family meeting in progress.

Mr. Kiersey sat as if he might have been Raggedy Andy in a heap on the floor if he hadn't had the chair for support. "Anna is okay. If it hadn't been for Dr. Hamilton, she probably would have died."

"Wouldn't Trisha have known what to do?" Deedee asked.

"Trisha is a nurse. Her best abilities lie in knowing when an injury is serious enough to call an ambulance. But our facilities and knowledge are usually quite limited. She can treat the usual camp casualties."

"But this isn't a usual camp casualty," Deedee agreed. She put her face in her hands for a moment, then looked to her father for more information.

Mr. Kiersey wiped a tear trying to escape. "When I asked Dr. Hamilton to come here, I knew he wasn't happy. But it sure was God's leading, wasn't it?"

Joseph nodded emphatically. Eve sat wide-eyed, not moving.

"Dr. Hamilton knew that the most crucial tactic in a scalp wound is to stop the bleeding. He explained to me the only way to stop the bleeding in that type of wound is to stitch it up immediately. Any of the rest of us would have been worried about bear germs, dirt, and hair in the way." Mr. Kiersey shook his head. His voice got husky and quiet. "God took care of my little girl."

Adam jumped up from his place on the floor and stomped over to his father. "If God took care of Anna, why'd the bear bite her in the first place?"

Mr. Kiersey put his hands out to hold his son by his arms. Adam wrestled away in anger. "I don't know why the bear would bite her. And I don't think God wanted that to happen. We live in a world where bad things happen."

"So God doesn't really take care of us?" Adam demanded.

"Bad things happen, Adam. We can't stop them if we've made a bad choice that makes it happen. But what God does is hold our hand through every awful thing. He doesn't let us go through it alone. He also takes us from that bad thing Satan meant to hurt us with and makes something good out of it."

"Oh, sure," Adam spouted, "I'm never going to be happy about this."

Mr. Kiersey's face softened. "Did I say good is always happy? It's not, Adam. It's good for you to take medicine when you're sick. But it's not happy to take medicine. Sometimes what is good for us is something difficult.

"God allowed all of us free choice. We can choose to obey God or Satan or what we want to do. He doesn't stop that free choice from happening. And when someone makes a bad choice and we happen to be in the way, we get hurt."

Adam plopped himself on his dad's lap and hid his

face in his shoulder. Mr. Kiersey put his arm around his son and continued talking to the other kids. "Mom and Anna will come home sometime tomorrow. Obviously Anna won't feel good. But we'll all love her and take care of her, won't we?"

China and Deedee got the kids to bed while Mr. Kiersey talked on the phone. They heard the story over and over, wafting up the stairs into the rooms of the children as he called grandparents and friends and church for prayer support. Eve clung to them as they tried to put her to bed. "Please don't let me sleep alone. I'm scared. I'm scared the bear's going to get me."

"The bear won't get you," Deedee reassured. "They don't want to come into the house."

China shuddered, thinking about the broken Eela-puash kitchen door. *They said these bears don't bite. Don't attack humans. And they did. They were strong enough to break into the kitchen. So why wouldn't they come in here?*

"I still don't want to sleep alone," Eve whimpered, starting to cry. "I miss Anna."

Deedee looked at China, sizing her up, trying to say something with her eyes. As if looking to see what kind of friend China was.

China pulled the little girl close. "We all miss Anna. Why don't you sleep with Deeds and I tonight?"

Deedee smiled at her friend. "You're the best," she whispered.

CHAPTER FOURTEEN

THE GIRLS PUT EVE IN DEEDEE'S BED, tucked her in and turned on a tape for Eve. They promised to come up shortly.

Mr. Kiersey sat in his chair, his hand covering his face. As they came in the room, he moved his hand away and looked at them blankly. Deedee went to hug him. "Are you telling the truth, Daddy? Will Anna be okay?"

He nodded. "At least physically. Who knows what a trauma like that will do to such a little girl."

The aching pain inside China swelled. She tasted an awful burning liquid that bubbled up in her throat. She swallowed hard. If she stayed in the room one more second, she knew she'd fall apart. "Anyone want hot chocolate?" China asked, disappearing into the kitchen.

"We'll be having a visitor shortly," Mr. Kiersey said.

"I'll make four mugs."

"Thanks, China. You've been such a help."

Deedee's voice. "Who's coming, Daddy?"

"The ranger."

"Why the ranger?"

"He needs a full report from you girls. I hope that's okay."

China stirred the chocolate into the warming milk. *I don't want to remember. I don't ever want to talk about it. See the blood. And I never want to see another bear again.*

The ranger arrived in time for hot chocolate. He sat comfortably in the rocker, facing the girls. Although the sofa was big enough for four, China and Deedee huddled together.

The ranger began without any social niceties. "This is highly unusual that bears would attack a human. These bears are normally afraid of people. But it is also unusual for them to travel in pairs."

"We heard your talk," Deedee offered.

"We thought it unusual for bears to even approach the boys sleeping outside, but we decided that the amount of sweet food on their hands was too much for the bears. We also took into account the fact they had just raided the kitchen so close by."

"And the boy yanked his hand out of the bear's mouth," Deedee reminded him.

The ranger nodded. "But that yank did produce some blood."

"So why would a bear attack a little girl?" China asked.

"That's why I'm here. To try to figure that out. No matter what, I need a good, detailed description of the bears. I saw them the other day but wanted to make sure the ones who bit your sister were the same ones."

"They were the same ones," China affirmed. "Two. A big one and a little one."

"The little one didn't do it," Deedee said.

The ranger prodded them to tell the story. China held onto her warm mug, hoping that would give her strength to get through it. To see it all over again. To smell the blood. To smell the bear and his horrible stench. To hear Anna and Eve's screams. To be more scared than she'd ever been in her entire life.

The ranger gently asked questions, without asking some of the gory details. China somehow got through.

Deedee ran her fingers through her hair, as if getting up enough courage to ask. "What do you think made them do this?"

The ranger set his mug down on the small lamp table next to the rocker. "Bears have a natural fear of man..."

The girls nodded, listening intently.

"... the only thing that seems to break this fear is when they eat man's food."

"Isn't that good?" China asked. "If they aren't afraid of us, then we could coexist happily."

The ranger shook his head emphatically. "Remember that I told you bears think of food, food, and more food?"

The girls nodded again.

"If bears lose their fear of man, then they look on man as food. They aren't afraid of the little critters in the forest, so they eat them. If they are afraid of something, they won't eat it, they'll run away. If they aren't afraid, it becomes food."

China thought her stomach had crawled into her chest. At the same time, it fell into her shoes. *This can't be . . .*

Deedee pushed off her shoes, then sat cross-legged on the sofa. "So how does a bear stop being afraid of man?"

"Like I said, if they eat our food. Bears know food by the smell. If they eat garbage, for example, they smell man's scent on the food. The next time they look for food, they equate the scent of man with something that tastes good . . . even if it isn't man they tasted."

China felt faint. The room began to take little dips and twists. She swallowed hard and clutched the arm of the sofa.

Deedee's voice sounded thin and stretched. "But if they tasted blood on that boy, wouldn't that give them the taste for blood?"

"Possibly. But it's more likely they've somehow gotten garbage. The fact that they were not afraid to come so close to a group of people in order to eat those taxidermied animals leads us to believe someone fed them and probably fed them well."

Deedee clutched China's arm.

"The night of the accident, we found bear tracks and pieces of garbage in the clearing not too far from this house."

"WHAT?" bellowed Mr. Kiersey. "That's the first I've heard about this."

Tears began to well up and drip down China's face. "Do you mean feeding the bears garbage would cause them to attack a human?"

The ranger nodded. "As far as we can tell. But why he would attack that particular child, I'm not sure. Did she have any food smells on her hands? Had she had a snack? Been around a barbecue fire?"

Deedee shook her head. "We remembered what you had said, making her wash her hands. She'd had a bath right before, but we made her wash her hands again."

China began to sob so hard she could hardly get her words out. "But she smelled like . . . like . . . watermelon."

The ranger looked confused. "Why would she smell like watermelon?"

Deedee, stunned, answered. "Her shampoo smells like watermelon. Whenever we wash her hair, it smells just like at the watermelon feed when the juice is spilling all over the tables. It's as if there were such things as watermelon flowers and they're in full bloom."

The ranger made a note in his book. "That would

do it. Now, if we could just find out who fed the bears..."

China had never felt so much guilt in her entire life. *I almost killed Anna. The sweet, precious baby. I almost killed her! Oh God, oh God, oh God. Dr. Hamilton was right. I'm no good. I'm stupid. I wish the bear had bit me.* She couldn't stop crying long enough to tell the ranger. Her heart screamed, *IT WAS ME!*

The ranger went on, "We have to find them and kill them as soon as possible."

"Kill who?" Deedee asked tightening her grip on China's arm.

"The bears."

Mr. Kiersey spoke up. "Can't you just move them somewhere else?"

The ranger shook his head. "They will travel 50 miles to a place where they know they can get food. And once they've attacked humans, they must absolutely be destroyed."

China's sobs grew harder, she wanted so much to tell him. She wanted the ranger to shoot her instead of the bears. Between sobs, she finally managed to squeak it out. "It...was...my...fault."

Deedee's sobs joined China's, "Daddy, we almost had Anna killed. We didn't mean to."

"And...now...the...innocent bears...will... have...to die...too," China gasped between sobs.

Mr. Kiersey looked at the girls. "What do you mean?"

Deedee spoke. "Dr. Hamilton was so mean and awful to us. He said teenagers were worthless. We wanted to prove to him that maybe we could do something out of the ordinary."

"What does that have to do with bears?" Mr. Kiersey demanded.

"We thought if we could tame them . . ." At that moment, China knew how stupid an idea that had been.

"But I told you never to let the bears get to our garbage!" Mr. Kiersey said, his anger beginning to ooze out. "Why didn't you obey me?"

"But Daddy," Deedee protested, "You never told me why. You just said, 'Don't feed the bears and don't let them get into our garbage.' I thought that meant they made a big mess with the garbage. And I wasn't stupid enough to feed them by hand."

Mr. Kiersey's anger disappeared as fast as it had come.

Deedee continued, since China cried too hard to say anything. "We heard if you feed them they lose their fear of man. But no one said that meant they thought of us as food."

The ranger looked at his notebook. Mr. Kiersey looked at his daughter. "Deedee, when I give an order I expect it to be obeyed, whether you understand the reasons why or not."

Kemper suddenly stood before China in her mind. She could see him on stage. She could hear Dr.

Hamilton talking about unquestioning obedience. And Kemper telling the kids how we have to obey God ... sometimes without knowing why. Her head dropped forward into her hands. *I told you I'd obey you, God. No questions asked. I guess I should have obeyed Mr. Kiersey, too.*

CHAPTER FIFTEEN

CHINA RINSED OUT THE MUGS and left them in the sink. Her tears kept flowing as if someone had turned on the faucet and forgot to turn it off. Her heart hurt. Someone had taken it out, played squash with it, then stuffed it back inside her chest. Her mind pounded accusations. Never, never in her life had she wished she hadn't been born. No matter how awful things got, or what decisions she made, she never wished she hadn't been born. Until now.

Eve slept on her back, one arm around her stuffed frog, the other over her head. The sheet dangled off the side of the bed, covering only one foot. China lifted the sheet and covered the little girl. She didn't stop to wipe the tears. Why bother? More came quickly to replace those wiped away.

Deedee moved about the room like a puppet doll whose strings were held by an amateur. Her movements jerky and indecisive. She pulled off her shorts and flopped on a blanket on the floor without taking her shirt off.

China looked around the room for something to sleep on.

"Your sleeping bag was ruined," Deedee stated flatly.

"It wasn't mine," China said.

"And your pillow."

"I don't want it."

China wandered around, lost in the small room.

"Blankets are in the upstairs hallway closet."

China curled up on the hardwood floor. "I don't want to go out there again."

Deedee said nothing. China moved around, trying to get comfortable. She sat up, her back against the bed. She caught her breath. "Do you hate me?"

Deedee didn't move. Didn't speak.

"I hate myself."

Silence.

China put her head in her hands, wanting to pray. Wanting to talk to God. But feeling like He didn't want to talk to her. She could see His back turned. If He wasn't such an adult He'd probably have His fingers in His ears, too. He didn't want to hear from her.

"Deeds," she whispered. "I'm so, so, sorry. I'll go back to Guatemala now."

Deedee said nothing. She didn't move. China couldn't even hear her breathing. Eve's tiny slumbering breaths were the only sound in the room.

China got up and left the room. She tiptoed down the hall, up the stairs, and into Eve and Anna's room.

She lay down on Anna's bed and began to cry. Somehow, sometime, the tears stopped and exhaustion took over.

A tall silhouette stood in the doorway. The yellow light from the hall created a glowing halo around him. She had fallen asleep on her stomach, with her hands underneath her face. She opened her eyes and looked at Mr. Kiersey without moving another muscle. He didn't move either. But he must have seen her eyes open. He must know he had wakened her.

"I'm sorry, China," he said softly. His head went down. His fingers pinched the bridge of his nose. China had to squint her eyes against the sudden light. His head moved slowly from side to side. Then to himself he wailed, *"Why* didn't I think to explain things?"

China's eyes adjusted to the light. She didn't move. She just watched. She hadn't a clue what to say anyway. What do you say when "sorry" doesn't even come close to being enough?

Mr. Kiersey turned and leaned against the doorjamb. "On the one hand, I can't believe what you've done. On the other, I don't put all the blame on you."

"How could you not blame me?" China whispered, tears spilling out again.

Mr. Kiersey walked over to Eve's bed and sat on it, facing China. "I'm so frustrated, angry, and confused about this whole thing. But I can't put all fault on you. I never explained things to Deedee. Since I understood what the rangers meant, I assumed everyone else did, too. I could have been more clear. I could have made certain Deedee understood."

"I could have obeyed what you told Deedee," China said softly.

"Yes, you should have obeyed or at least asked questions if you didn't understand."

"I thought I did understand," China said, sounding lame even to herself.

Mr. Kiersey's fingertips did spider push-ups against each other. "At the very least, I think there should be consequences for your disobedience."

China nodded.

"Did you think you were disobeying? Did you go directly against my wishes?"

China sat up in the bed, pulling the sheet up to her chin. She shook her head. "No. I never meant to disobey. I thought I understood the dangers and that I was not doing anything dangerous."

A weak smile briefly touched Mr. Kiersey's face. He patted her foot. "That's why I don't put all the fault on you. You acted out of typical teenage logic."

China winced.

"I should have thought of that when I gave my kids a bear talk. But then, we've never had bear problems here before. I guess the several years of drought are finally pushing them down the mountain to find food and water." He reached up to tweak her nose. "But next time you want to deal with something so big and potentially dangerous, why don't you ask a few more questions."

China nodded.

"I want you and Deedee to think of what you feel are appropraite consequences for what you did. This is a very, very serious thing, China. I don't want you to minimize it."

China shook her head. "I don't, Mr Kiersey. I wouldn't even be surprised if you sent me home."

"I don't think you'd learn anything from that. Think of consequences in what this family calls the 'Three Ps'. Consequences that are positive, practical, and pertain to what happened." Mr. Kiersey stood and kissed her on the top of her head. "Go to sleep now, China."

China slid back down in the bed. She lay there, no pillow under her head, staring at the ceiling. Re-runs covered with blood played across the ceiling. She scrunched her eyes shut against the pictures, but they played over again on the screen of her mind. "Please, God. Can you help me not think about it right now?" The pictures faded into smells of watermelon-scented wispy hair, and she fell asleep.

In the silent morning, China fed the boys and Eve while Deedee slept curled on the floor. China felt empty. She preferred emptiness to the accusing words flying about her head.

Mr. Kiersey drank the last of his coffee. He put his mug in the sink and kissed China on the head again. "Diana will be home with Anna around noon. You can still get to work." China couldn't look at him. She watched his shoes instead. He chucked her under the chin, pulling it up until he could see her eyes. "I appreciate all you're doing around here, China. I wish you were one of my daughters."

I don't deserve to be anybody's daughter! China's mind screamed. She kept her mouth closed.

Adam flicked on the camp's shortwave radio to listen to the chatter. China blocked out most of it. Tim needed Joe to show up with the lumber to fix a cabin in the Main Camp. Administration was looking for Mr. Kiersey. Accomodations needed someone to buy more floor wax. The voices clicked off and on. Monotone. Issuing messages and orders in the same tone of voice. China wiped off the kitchen table, sweeping cereal and globs of oatmeal into her hand with a sponge. Deedee walked in, bleary-eyed, stumbling with sleep. She dropped into a chair and laid her head on the table, closing her eyes.

A new voice came over the radio waves. It caught China's attention immediately. "We've found them!" the voice fairly shouted. "Near the mud pit. We've got them treed."

Injected with instant energy, Deedee sat up straight. China sank down into a chair. Both watched the radio as if looking at it would help them listen better.

"We're on our way," a familiar voice responded. "Be careful."

"The ranger," Deedee said.

The girls watched the radio, waiting for more news. China's heart picked up its pace. She wiped her sweaty palms on her shorts. The only voices through the radio had the same, dribbling nonsense about maintenance-type stuff.

"We're coming up behind," the ranger's voice broke in.

"Do you see them in the pine?"

"Not yet."

"We've got both boys up there."

"Don't shoot," the ranger warned them. "The man with the license must dispatch them. No one else."

"No fair" came an almost inaudible voice over the radio.

China hadn't realized tears appeared again.

"Move east," the ranger ordered.

"Ten-four."

"We're ready to dispatch."

"Ten . . ." the gunshots came then. Two of them. Then the radio went silent.

CHAPTER SIXTEEN

CHINA STARED AT THE RADIO. She felt as if someone had taken cleats and marched all over her body. She bled now. Inside. Bled for the bears. "I killed them," she said to no one in particular.

"We both did" came Deedee's painful reply.

"It was me. I sucked you into this." China sat with her hands folded, staring at how white they got when she squeezed them. Squeezing her hands was the only way she could hold herself together.

The front door flew open. "Kemper's here!" Adam announced.

Kemper's huge form filled the doorway. Without an invitation he moved toward the sofa and sat down. China moved to the other end. As far away from him as she could. Deedee got up from the kitchen table and sat in her dad's chair. "Hi, Kemper," she managed to say.

Kemper looked from one girl to the other, slapping his slim Bible gently on his leg.

"We killed the bears," China said, her eyes filling with tears. She seemed to have an endless supply of hot, tormenting tears. "We almost killed Anna."

Kemper didn't tell them they hadn't. He didn't tell them not to worry about it. He sat there and nodded his head. A listening nod. An assent that he heard them.

Deedee ran her fingers through her hair, combing it. "Dr. Hamilton was right about teenagers. We're stupid and we're not worth anything."

Kemper nodded some more. "I'm not surprised you feel that way." Then he shook his head. "It's an awful, horrible, totally helpless and hopeless feeling."

Some of the ugliness started to leak out of China. Kemper just sitting there and listening poked a hole in the festering wound and allowed it to drain. He reached over to hold China's hand. She melted in the warm love she felt through his grasp.

They sat there like that awhile. Then Deedee pulled the rocker over to the other side of Kemper and held his other hand.

Kemper squeezed their hands. China couldn't believe it. She could swear his eyes filled with tears. He let go of China's hand and wiped underneath his eyes. "I thought I killed my sister. I still wonder if it was my fault she died."

Deedee spoke softly. "But I thought she had some kind of disease."

"She did. But I was responsible to watch her that

day. And when she started having trouble, I didn't see the signs enough to think I should call an ambulance. I thought she was just having a little coughing fit. I always wonder what would have happened if I had called the ambulance."

The girls didn't respond.

Kemper rubbed China's hand. He looked at the floor. "The doctor said it was time for her to die. He said that over and over. But I could never get past the thought that maybe, if I had done something different, she would still be alive."

China wanted to reassure him he hadn't done anything stupid. But she couldn't say that. She didn't know. But she realized he knew how she felt. And a tiny light of hope began to shine.

Kemper let go of the girls' hands and took on his teacher look. "I didn't come here to tell you not to hurt. Or not to accept responsibility for anything you might have done wrong. That's between you and God. But when you logically look at your responsibility, I want you to accept it, confess it, then let it go. Don't dwell on the 'if onlys'. They can destroy you if you let them."

Kemper flipped open his Bible to Romans 8:28. "God works all things together for good for them that love him and are called according to His purpose."

Deedee groaned. "Don't throw that verse at me, Kemper. There's nothing good about what's happened here. Two bears are dead and Anna is badly hurt because of our stupidity. There is nothing good."

"Good isn't always happy," Kemper reminded her.

"Oh, shut up." Deedee jumped from the rocker and ran to her room.

China patted his arm. "I'm sorry about your sister, Kemper. But it doesn't seem like anything good can come from this at all." She put her head down onto her hand to try to push away the headache.

Kemper stood and touched her shoulder. "Pray that God will help you find something good."

Kemper let himself out the front door, closing the screen with only a whisper of metallic whine from the hinge.

Unfamiliar tires rolled over the gravel drive. Adam, the lookout, stuck his head inside the front door. "Anna's home!" The door slammed and Adam was gone.

China ran down the hallway. "Deedee. Anna's home."

Deedee pushed past China and ran out the front door. China sat on the sofa, waiting. Wanting to remain in her place. She folded her hands in her lap. Trembling.

Joseph pushed open the screen door and held it there. Deedee entered carrying a wrapped bundle as if all the fragile treasure of the world were inside. She sat on the rocker, closed her eyes, and held the bundle close.

Mrs. Kiersey came in next. Her eyes swollen and red. Her clothes rumpled. Her hair limp and oily. She acknowledged China with a look, then moved down the hallway.

Dr. Hamilton strode into the room as if it were one of his operating theaters. His presence demanded attention and command. "Aside from minor scarring, she's going to have side effects."

"Like what, doctor?" Deedee asked.

"Headaches for awhile. But mostly emotional problems."

"Emotional?" China said under her breath. *I hadn't thought of that."*

"Night terrors . . ."

"You mean bad dreams?" Deedee asked.

"Nightmares are nothing compared to night terrors. She'll wake screaming. Nothing will be able to calm her."

China's breathing became short, choppy. She looked at the bundle.

"She'll probably regress in some of her development. Any talking might cease. She'll need diapers again. No telling how this has changed her."

He glared at one girl and then the other. "You should have thought of this before you put her in danger."

China stood up, her fists clenched. "We didn't intend to put her in danger . . ."

Dr. Hamilton shook his head. "No one ever does. But they march forward in their stupidity as though nothing else matters but themselves. Self is the only interest here, isn't it?"

"No!" China fairly screamed. "If you hadn't been so pigheaded rude, maybe we wouldn't have seen a need to try to show you not all teenagers are the same."

As soon as the words were out of her mouth, she wished she could shove them back in. A smirk spread across Dr. Hamilton's face. "Well now, you proved my point quite well, did you not?"

China clenched and unclenched her fists. Mentally she had to pry her jaws apart to speak. "Even you make mistakes, doctor. You said so the other night in the meeting." China's voice came out high and pinched.

"My mistaken decisions were never the result of bullheaded stupidity. Mine followed carefully calculated, well-thought-out options . . . of which I happe ·d to possibly choose the wrong one. But in my work, one can never be certain their choice was, in fact, wrong. Eternity will tell."

"B-b-but, you said . . ." China protested.

"Less than a handful of mistakes, Miss Tate. And they were not—I repeat—were not a result of frivolous behavior." Without waiting for China to respond, Dr. Hamilton strode over to his patient, looked in her eyes, then very tenderly kissed the top of her head. "Anna's a great patient," he said to her with a genuine smile. The smile faded as he unfolded himself to his full height. "I've left written instructions with your mother, Deedee. If you don't think you can obey them explicitly, I would suggest you let your mother care for your sister."

At the door, he turned to face China one more time. "You know, Heather was right. You take a challenge to the extreme just to prove you are right. You'd be better off just accepting the perception others have of you. I think they have a better perspective of you than you have of yourself." With that final dig, he let himself out the door.

China plopped back onto the sofa. Deedee had her face buried in the little bundle, oblivious to the world around her. The rocker creaked with every backward motion. "How is she, Deedee?"

"She's hurt," Deedee snapped.

China got up and went over to her. She didn't know what she had expected Anna to look like. But she did know she didn't expect her to look like this. She had a round swollen face that looked like a sad jack-o-lantern. Although her whole face was discolored, she had a vicious bruise under her right eye. A gauzy hat sat on her head, protecting the wound. Instead of watermelon, she smelled like powerful antiseptic. "Can I hold her?"

"No!"

China walked out of the house. She didn't let the screen door slam. She didn't answer Eve's chattering questions as she passed. She walked without seeing or thinking through the forest, past the lake, and up to Eelapuash. She did let the new screen door on the kitchen crash shut behind her. Once inside, she wondered why she had come. She'd only make a disaster of things. She'd proven that over and over again.

She walked back outside, letting the door crash. Outside, the pain squeezed her heart. She needed something to hold. Someone to love her regardless of how stupid she'd been. She walked inside again, the door slamming a third time. She couldn't see a thing through her blurry, tear-filled eyes. So she stood, feeling like a helpless little girl.

"Where's the dog?" she called pitifully to anyone who might hear. "I want Bologna!"

CHAPTER SEVENTEEN

MAGDA CAME AROUND THE CORNER, untying her apron. She put her arm around China and walked her outside. "You come with me, China honey."

China walked along obediently. They walked down the path toward the bridge. Just before they got there, Magda ducked into the trees, pulling China along behind. She sat China down on a rock, facing the mountain. "Only three weeks ago I met a young lady here who had a world of hope in her eyes. And now that hope is gone."

"She's not a young lady. She's just a stupid idiot who can't do anything right."

Magda made a sound that sounded like a "Humph!" She shook her head. "I don't believe that for one minute. I've seen her heart and I know that it's a good one. Remember King David messed up awful bad and God said he was a 'man after God's own heart.' It don't take perfection to be a person after God's heart."

China turned to look at Magda. "King David had

someone killed."

Magda nodded. "No kidding. An innocent man. And he killed him after he stole the guy's wife and got her pregnant."

China looked at the mountain. She felt God looking at her, hoping she'd talk to Him. She realized He had not turned His back on her. She had turned away from Him because she was so ashamed.

"So, Magda, how do I make everything all right?"

"You don't," she said matter-of-factly.

"Oh, great. Thanks a lot."

"Only God can do that kind of thing. You only have to be repentant—that means be truly sorry and ask forgiveness of everyone whose been wronged here. Then you just have to be open in case God wants you to do somethin' else, too." Magda paused, drinking in the beauty around her. "It's not that you'd be doin' somethin' to make up for what happened. That ain't never gonna be. It would just be somethin' God can do since you're wiser now."

"Am I? I don't feel like it. I feel more stupid."

"If you lie in the mud and wallow, yep, I'd say you're more stupid. But if you've learned anything from this, get out of the mud, wash off, and get goin'. As a friend always told me, 'There's no sin in falling down. Only in lying there and wallowing in it . . . and not learning from your mistakes.'"

Magda stood slowly. "I've got to get back to the kitchen. Them kids is going to stampede if I don't get their food out in time."

China put her hand out for Magda to stop. "Does Rick hate me?"

"No, China honey. No one hates you. Everyone hurts for you."

"Not Dr. Hamilton."

Magda sighed. "When we make a mistake, not everyone can be forgiving. It's too bad. But I ain't gonna tell you nothin' but the truth."

China smiled. "I know, Magda. Thanks."

China stayed on her rock, looking at the mountains, thinking about what Magda had said. A slow smile came across her face. *God, I have learned a lot. Can you help me put what I've learned to good use?*

Inside the prayer chapel, China removed her shoes and talked to God in the quiet, darkened coolness. She took the responsibility for her part in the destruction. She asked for forgiveness and made a mental list of the others she would talk to. When she left, the burden from her heart was gone. The pain for Anna hadn't left, but the crushing ache of stupidity had vanished. And she knew what she could do to make sure no tragedy like this could ever happen again in camp.

❧

Two days later, China stood in front of 500 people in the Main Camp of Camp Crazy Bear. Deedee stood next to her. They momentarily linked pinkies before

China stepped up to the podium. Her knees trembled. The consequences — positive, practical, and certainly pertinent to what had happened — lay before her in the sea of faces. She and Deedee would be thoroughly educated in the habits and behavior of California black bears, and then they would educate others, starting right now.

"California Black Bears are not native to these mountains," China began hesitantly. She looked at her notes. "But they have lived here for about 30 years. So they think it's their home. Last week two of these bears had to die and a little girl was critically hurt because someone didn't understand the rules. But that doesn't have to happen any more. From now on, Camp Crazy Bear has two certified bear instructors. Me, China Tate, and Deedee Kiersey. After our presentation, if anyone has questions, please ask. And if you don't understand something, please clarify what you don't understand. That's what we're here for."

Deedee reached over to her friend's hand and squeezed it. China smiled, remembering what Deedee had said when she had asked for forgiveness, then suggested they educate the new summer campers every week. "You're all right, China Jasmine Tate. You can make a doozy of a mistake. But you make one heck of a friend."

JOIN CHINA IN EACH UNFORGETTABLE ADVENTURE

Get ready for more action! Life in the United States is very different from what China is used to in Guatemala. She's enjoying her independence and is always ready for fun and adventure. Come along with her to Camp Crazy Bear as she makes new friends and learns important biblical truths.

SLICED HEATHER ON TOAST

Heather Hamilton, the snobby camp beauty, has it in for China from their very first encounter. It soon turns into a week-long war of practical jokes— and valuable lessons.

THE SECRET IN THE KITCHEN

Now an employee of Camp Crazy Bear, China and her friend, Deedee, adopt a deaf stray dog. . . even though it's against camp rules. Meanwhile, some- one's planning a devious scheme that could cause great danger for China!

Available at your favorite Christian bookstore.

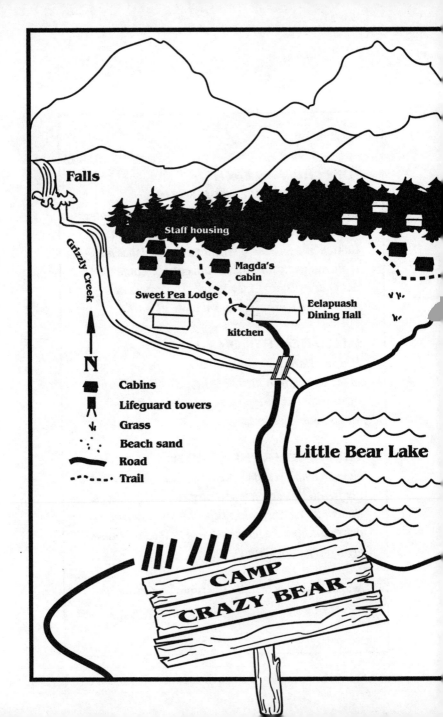

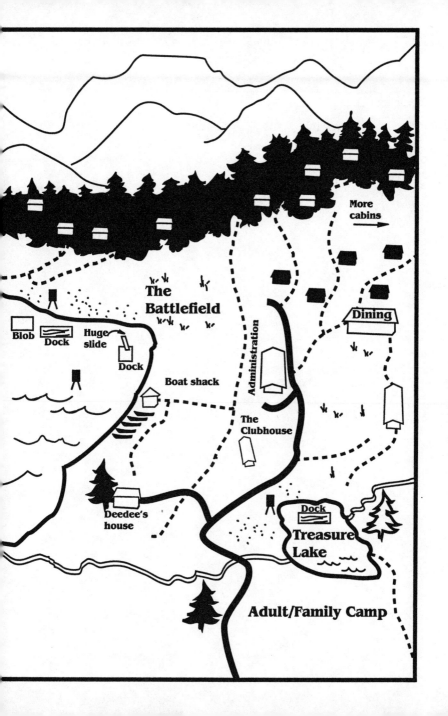